Fearghas
The McClains
Kirsten Osbourne

Chapter One

S cotland, 1530

Along with the rest of the village, Caitlin hurried to the keep to go to the wedding of the sixth son of the Laird of Clan McClain. Murdoch was the lad all the girls had wanted for their own—everyone but Caitlin, who had no desire to marry any of the laird's family. The family was just a wee bit odd, and she had no desire to be part of it.

The wedding of one of the sons of the laird was always fun, though, and the parties lasted for many hours. Caitlin had little time to party as she was raising her younger siblings. Her parents had been killed in the black plague when she was but a lass and the laird had brought her to the village to raise them, to make things easier for her.

Her father had always been a strong supporter of Laird McClain, but she was convinced that it was because he didn't know the laird well. Her younger brother and sister were now twelve and thirteen, and she knew they would be somewhere at the wedding, but she never knew where. They were wild children, and though she'd made an effort to tame them over the years, nothing had worked.

She got to the keep just in time to watch the bride descend the long staircase and join her groom at the bottom of the stairs. The vows were exchanged, and Caitlin couldn't help but rejoice. The bride—Lilli—had been a good friend of Caitlin's for a long time, and she was so happy to see her friend marry the man she loved. Lilli had often tried to get her to spend time with Fearghas, the youngest of the laird's sons, and the future laird of the clan, but Caitlin simply couldn't be around the laird's family without feeling uncomfortable.

After the wedding, there was a huge feast, and they all ate something the laird called tacos. It was an odd meal, but one the laird's family loved, and they were served at most of the parties that took place in the keep.

Once the dancing started, Caitlin stood off to one side, clapping and tapping her toes, but not really dancing with any men. Nay, her siblings were too much of a chore for most men to be willing to even look at her, much less ask her to dance.

So she was surprised when she felt a tapping at her shoulder. "Dance with me," Fearghas, the laird's youngest son, said.

"I thank ye, but nay. I must keep an eye on my younger brother and sister."

"They'll be fine. I don't see them here anyway." He took her hand and led her to the dance floor, moving into a traditional Scot'Tish dance, the step dance.

"I'm afraid I don't know much about dancing. There's been little time for frivolity in me life."

"Then it's time you begin now, isn't it?"

She carefully watched his feet and mimicked the dance he was doing, though they thankfully didn't need to touch for this dance. It was more about the way their feet moved to the music.

By the end of the dance, she was laughing softly, as she'd been spectacularly unable to keep up, and had made something of a fool of herself. He was grinning, looking happy as can be. As they left the dance floor, he smiled at her. "I promised me brother Murdoch that I would dance with ye at his wedding."

"Why me?" she asked, a bit surprised.

"Because he married your dear friend. He told me that they've been wanting us to do things with them, but that ye always refused. Why is that?"

She sighed, biting her lip. She had to come up with a good excuse that had nothing to do with how very odd his family was. "I'm raising me brother and sister. I haven't had time for courtship or much else that would be considered fun."

"I see. And if I said I wanted to court you?"

"I...would respectfully decline." Caitlin didn't want to anger Fearghas, but it didn't seem like a good idea to enter into any kind of relationship with him.

"What if I promised to have someone to care for your siblings? Would that make things better?"

She shook her head. "Nay. You'll soon be laird, and I'm just a country girl. My father had cattle, and he sold milk to the neighboring farms. There is no way I could be courted by our future laird."

"This future laird finds himself enamored of you. Walk with me, and I'll plead my case."

She was tempted to spend more time with him. He had always seemed like someone she would enjoy being with, but his family was just...she couldn't put her finger on what was wrong with them, but it felt as if there was something truly wrong, and she didn't need that. But if she said no, would that cause his family to be unhappy with her and her siblings? She didn't know what the right thing to do was.

"Aye, I'll walk with ye." She agreed against her better judgment, but she certainly didn't want her younger siblings to suffer because of her stubbornness.

He offered her his arm as they got outside. It was spring, and the weather was beautiful. "So you're raising your brother and sister?"

She nodded. "Aye. My parents were killed by the plague. Father was a farmer, and we were a long ride from the village. By the time I sent for a healer, it was too late. So yer father moved me here with my brother and sister, and I've been responsible for them ever since."

"I'm sorry you lost your parents. I know my family did all they could, and we lost no one in the village."

"That always struck me as odd. Other doctors throughout Europe were unable to cure the plague, but even though it came through the village, the healers in your family were able to fight it off? How can that be?"

He paused for a moment, and began walking again. His mind was obviously conflicted about something. "Me family is a bit different than most. That's all I can really say, but the differences we have make us good at things others are sometimes not."

"What does that mean?"

"I canna tell ye more. I hate that I must keep this secret, but I can only explain to me future wife. You wouldn't want to be me wife, would ye?"

She laughed softly. "Does that mean Lilli knows?"

He frowned. "Aye, she knows, but she also knows she mustn't tell anyone."

If anyone could get the secret out of Lilli, Caitlin knew she could. Though Lilli was pretty good about not telling secrets. "As the leaders of our clan, dinna ye think it's important ta tell yer people what is different about ye?"

"Not at all. It's not safe for our secret to be out. I'm sorry, lass. I wish I could tell ye, but I was sworn to secrecy before I could even write me name."

"At least ye write. I wasna close enough to the town school to learn."

"I could teach you," he said softly, and she glanced at him with surprise.

"Why are ye being so kind to me?"

"My brother's wife is your closest friend. I need to get to know you better. So I shall teach ye to read and write."

Caitlin could make no sense of him. Why would he feel the need to get to know her better, simply because his brother married her friend? "Tell me more about your family."

Fearghas frowned. "We are a healthy lot, who live long lives," he said. "We came here from England many generations ago, and we agreed to lead the clan. Me family has been the leaders of the clan ever since. Me grandfather tells me that we used the name Clain in England, and took on the name McClain after moving here."

"I didn't know any of that. So your family isn't truly Scot?"

He chuckled. "With as long as we've lived here, I promise you, we're Scots through and through."

She smiled at that. "And why does the youngest son always become laird?"

"In me family, every seventh son has seven sons. It has always been a family tale that the seventh son of a seventh son is lucky beyond belief. So it makes sense to us that the seventh son would be the one to rule."

She thought about that for a moment before nodding. "I can understand that."

He stopped walking abruptly. "Adder."

Her foot was in the air, and when she looked down, she could see she was about to step on the adder. In slow motion, she watched her foot descend, but then the snake was in half, bleeding out onto the ground. "What happened?" she asked.

"I don't know," he said, and deep down, she knew he was lying to her. He knew exactly what had happened.

"I've never seen an adder split in half when stepped on. That makes no sense whatsoever."

"It is odd."

"You made it happen, didn't you? That's one of the strange things about your family. So many odd things happen when you're around."

"If you say," he said simply.

"Fearghas, why won't you tell me the truth?"

"'Tis not my truth to tell."

As they kept walking, she realized that she was attracted to him, which was exactly the opposite of what she wanted. "I think your family should be honest about how they do things."

"Perhaps," he said. "But I think keeping it in the family is what's necessary. If you want to know the secret badly enough, you'll marry me."

She laughed. "Sure. The orphan who is raising her siblings will marry the future laird. That makes no sense."

"I choose who I marry. No one else does."

"Your mother would have a fit."

He laughed. "You really don't know anything about my family. My mother feels it's her duty to get me married off, so she and father can stop being laird and lady of the clan. She would be open to us marrying this evening if we would agree."

"Nay," she said simply. How could she think about marrying into a family with so many secrets? "But I thank you for saving me from the adder."

Fearghas simply looked at her for a moment. "Yer quite welcome, lass."

"So you admit you saved me?" Caitlin asked.

"When I deny it, you question my honesty. When I admit it, you question me. What does a man have to do to get you to believe him?"

She shrugged. "I'm not sure yet, but I'll let you know when I am."

As they rounded the loch, she caught sight of her sister in the woods with a boy Caitlin had forbidden her to spend time with. "Marta! Come here this instant!"

Marta saw her sister, and she hung her head. "Caitlin, we're just talking."

"That's not what I saw," Caitlin called back. She was quite exasperated with her sister.

Marta hurried out of the woods and to the edge of the loch. "Why can't I be with a boy?"

"You can. In full sight of the entire village. Not slinking away into the woods with him!"

"But Caitlin! He's asked if he can court me."

"And I said no!"

Fearghas stood listening for a moment, and he realized that Caitlin needed support with this younger sister of hers. "Go into the keep and join the festivities. There will be no more time alone in the woods with boys."

"'Tis not fair!" Marta complained, but she turned and ran to the keep.

"Thank ye again," Caitlin said, wondering where they'd find her brother, Aileen. He was the youngest of the three of them, and hands down, the most mischievous.

"Ye need help."

Caitlin shrugged. "I never said otherwise. Unfortunately, there is no one not involved with their own family. My siblings are my responsibility."

And then she spotted Aileen. He was hiding in the woods with another boy, and she could see smoke. "Aileen! What are ya doin?"

Aileen tried to blow out the small fire he'd created, managing only to fan it and make it burn higher.

Fearghas ran toward the woods, and stomped on the fire, while making a strange motion with his hands that looked as if he was covering something with a cupping motion.

The fire was out instantly. "Do ye realize we'd have all been in danger if that fire had grown?"

"Sorry," Aileen looked down at his feet, but Caitlin knew better. The boy was anything but contrite.

She was ready to scream. She hadn't taken time to simply enjoy herself in ages, and the first time she tried, her siblings ran wild. What was she to do with them?

"Aileen. Go back to the cottage and wait for me. I'll be there once I've sorted Marta out. Why can't the two of you do as you're told and stay put?"

Aileen hung his head as he headed back to the cottage, and Fearghas looked at the boy he'd been with. "Go to your mother now. Or I will."

The boy ran off to find his mother. Fearghas looked at Caitlin. "I know you think my family is too secretive, but you need help with the children. You must marry me."

She shook her head. "I can't marry someone who keeps so many secrets."

"Aye, you can, and you will. As the future laird of this clan, I demand it. I will help you raise the children, and you will be able to enjoy yourself without always worrying about them."

"You canna order me to marry you!"

"I just did! I can ask me father to order it if you don't want to take orders from me!"

"There is no need to drag the laird into this! I have taken care of the children for years. You can't step in now and refuse to let me finish the task."

"I can and I have. I will ask me mother to start the wedding plans immediately."

"Nay! I have a say in who I marry!"

He caught her by the waist and pulled her to him, stopping her protests with his kiss. She fought against him for a moment, and then she succumbed to his touch. There was no way she could marry a man who did nothing but make her angry. No, she needed to...she needed to keep kissing him.

Her arms went around his neck, and she kissed him back with all she had in her. With it being her first kiss, she had no idea what she was doing, but he seemed to know.

When he let go of her, she stared up at him, her eyes wide. "You will marry me, lass. Let's go and talk to my parents."

Following him was the last thing Caitlin wanted to do, while at the same time, what she wanted the most. How could this man leave her so confused?

Chapter Two

Caitlin followed Fearghas into the keep, and she took her sister's arm as soon as she saw her, pulling her along up the stairs, where they could look out over the celebration the clan was having. "Wait here!" Fearghas said, hurrying back down the stairs.

Marta looked at Caitlin. "What is he doing?"

"Getting his parents, I believe. He invited me for a walk, and we spotted both you and Aileen misbehaving. Fearghas, the future laird, saw that the two of you are too much for me to handle on my own, so he's telling me I must marry him."

Marta's eyes widened. "But you think the family is strange. You've always said you wouldn't marry into it if you were paid to do so."

"That's right. And now it looks like I'll be forced to marry him because of you running wild as you have. My whole life is changing, and I have no desire for this change!" Deep down, she knew she was lying. She felt a strange attraction toward Fearghas. She always had.

"I'm sorry," Marta looked down, and this time she truly seemed to be upset over her own actions.

Fearghas returned a moment later with both of his parents behind him. He briefly explained what had happened on their walk, and expressed his desire to marry Caitlin. "She needs the help. We should have been checking in with her to see how things were going, but it's too late to do so now." Fearghas shook his head. "I would like to marry her to help out with the two children."

His parents exchanged a look. "Yer certain?" his father asked.

Fearghas nodded once.

His mother looked at Caitlin. "Is this what you want?"

"Nay. I want to handle this myself."

Fearghas sighed. "Father, I would like you to order her to marry me."

"Nay!" his mother said, shaking her head. "I was almost forced to marry, and those were the worst days of my life. I came here and married your father instead, but then I felt the need to rescue my sister. You know I canna agree with this!"

"What are your objections to marrying my son?" Laird Duncan asked.

Caitlin took a deep breath, knowing that she had to admit to thinking the family strange, so this man wouldn't force her to marry his son. "During the time we have lived in the village, I've heard whispers about how odd your family is. The clan loves you and supports you, of course, but the oddities are noted and whispered about. I have no desire to marry into a family who is as odd as I've been told and observed myself."

Duncan nodded. "What oddities have you observed?"

"A few moments ago, I was walking with your son around the loch, and I was about to step on an adder. Fearghas did something, and I have no idea what, but the adder split in half before my foot touched it."

Duncan looked at his son who was frowning. "I think ye'll have to marry me son. There's not another way to keep our secret." He looked at Lady Alana. "I do hope ye understand me love!"

Alana frowned, but nodded. "'Tis necessary. Get your brother and the marriage can take place today. We're already celebrating."

Caitlin knew she had no choice then. If Lady Alana hadn't agreed to her plea then no one would. "Marta, go and fetch our brother."

Marta didn't have to be told twice, seeming to be confused by the entire conversation. "Aye." She ran down the stairs and out of the keep, and Caitlin knew her life would be forever changed.

Alana took Caitlin's hand. "Welcome to the family," she said softly.

"I thought you didn't want me to be forced into marriage," Caitlin said, wanting to know what had changed the woman's mind.

"Yes, but you saw too much, I'm afraid. You see, our family is different and odd, and all the other things people say about us. Every seventh son is born with a power. Fearghas can make things happen with a hand motion and intention. When he was two, he was able to kill a wolf approaching him with his hand motions."

"That doesn't make sense," Caitlin protested.

"Can you give any other reason the snake would have been cut in half just as you were about to step on it?"

"Nay, but..."

"Show her," Alana said to her son.

Fearghas thought for a moment. "Father, would you hand me your sword?"

His father smiled, removing the ceremonial sword at his hip. He moved well away, and held the sword with the hilt away from his body. Fearghas made a beckoning motion with his hand, and the sword moved across the space between them, as if it had legs.

"How?" Caitlin asked in a whisper.

"The same as the adder," Fearghas said. "Me father has powers as well. He has power over water."

"What does that mean?"

"You know how there are times when the loch freezes in the middle of the summer, and we can all use the ice to cool off?" Fearghas asked.

"Aye. 'Tis very odd."

"It's my father's power. We could walk down to the loch, and he could show you."

"Nay. I've seen more than enough for one day." Caitlin looked at Alana. "And all of your sons have these odd powers?"

"Nay. Only my seventh son. That's why the seventh son is the one to become laird. He always has a special power that makes him more capable than the rest," Alana said softly. "I know it is too much to try to understand, but it is true."

"There's more, isn't there?"

Fearghas nodded. "Much more. I'm sorry that we have to be so hurried in our marriage, but you need help with the children anyway. You know you do."

Caitlin sighed. "I dinna know what to do anymore."

"I know. We'll figure it out together."

Finally, she nodded. "I feel strange marrying someone so he can help me with the children."

"But that's not the only reason," Alana said. "By joining our family, you agree not to share our secrets."

"I would never!" Caitlin couldn't believe she was being forced to marry when her word that she wouldn't do what they worried about should be enough.

"I understand. But it's a hard secret to keep even when you have reason to keep it."

Caitlin understood on one level, but she still didn't want to marry a man who had magic and a strange family. Or was it one and the same? It was hard to know at that point.

Then she saw Marta climbing the stairs with Aileen. Aileen looked scared. As soon as the two were within speaking range, Caitlin explained that she would be marrying Fearghas.

"Is he moving to our cottage?" Aileen asked.

Caitlin realized that hadn't been discussed. She looked at Fearghas for the answer. "Nay, you'll be moving here. My parents will take your cottage."

Caitlin wanted to argue with him about his parents leaving, but she knew better. 'Twas how this family did things, and she wasn't about to change them, no matter how hard she tried.

Aileen made a face. "I dinna want to live in the keep!"

"You've no choice," Caitlin said angrily. "If the two of you had behaved, I wouldn't have to live in the keep either."

"'Tis not a bad place to live," Fearghas insisted. "You'll love it here. I grew up in this keep, and I've lived here all my days."

Aileen kicked at the stone floor of the keep. He was obviously annoyed that he had to stay there.

Alana frowned. "I think we should have the wedding now, while everyone is here. Then we'll enlist some of the villagers to clean out your house and bring your belongings here. We'll keep your pots and pans. That way we will be able to see to our own meals."

Caitlin couldn't believe how quickly her life and all decisions were being taken from her. And hadn't Alana said all the seventh sons had a seventh son with power? Did that mean she was expected to give birth to seven sons? Who could possibly think that was a good idea?

Moments later, she was descending the stairs toward Fearghas and her wedding. It seemed like madness to marry him, but then she remembered the way he'd kissed her. Surely that was worth something. Perhaps they had passion between them and would have a good marriage. She certainly hoped it would work that way. There would be nine children who would benefit from this marriage. She just had to remind herself that it would all be fine.

Many looked stunned to see her marrying Fearghas, but Lilli was beaming. Obviously, she was thrilled that Caitlin was marrying Fearghas, but Caitlin still didn't understand why her friend was so determined the two of them should marry. It made no sense.

She stood beside Fearghas and repeated her vows. Unsure how she'd managed to say anything that made sense, she gasped when the priest told Fearghas to kiss his bride. How had she forgotten that was part of the ceremony?

Fearghas smiled at her and lowered his head to hers, and once again, she found herself wrapped up in the passion of his kiss. She forgot about the crowd around them and gave herself over to him.

When he finally lifted his head, his lips went to her ear. "That's why we're marrying. No matter what happens with your siblings, I need you in my life."

She stared up at him, unable to quite comprehend his words. She'd been forced to marry him because she knew his secret, but now he was saying it was for another reason entirely. People were crushing in around them to congratulate them, and to congratulate Fearghas for becoming the new laird.

She was amazed at the sheer number of people who were happy for them. However, there was one woman who stood on the outskirts of the crowd, glaring at Caitlin. Caitlin didn't know the woman, whoever she was.

There was a great deal more dancing and merriment, but Caitlin was upstairs with her siblings. "I must stay here for the rest of the evening. You two need to go back to the cottage and pack up everything we own. Leave the kitchen supplies. Some men will be at the cottage in a short while to bring the things here."

Marta looked like she wanted to protest, but instead she nodded. "Yes, Caitlin."

Aileen still looked afraid to say anything, so he simply nodded, following Marta out of the keep.

Caitlin moved back to Fearghas's side and smiled. That was all she had to do all evening, she promised herself. Smiling was enough.

She spotted the odd woman who had been glaring at her twice more during the feast, and she couldn't help but wonder why the woman seemed to hate her, when she knew they'd never met.

Lady Alana and some of the other women who had married seventh sons pulled her into the parlor and shut the door behind them. "Ask us anything," Alana said.

"How long has this family had the powers?" Caitlin asked.

"The story that's been told is the family was in England. A seventh son from the Clain family had come over with William the Conquerors army. His seventh son then married a Saxon woman, who was the daughter of a woman who had powers that had come through her mother's line, and her two sisters had powers as well.

"Until that moment, the seventh son had luck at his back, but after that union, all seventh sons were born with a power as well. 'Tis said the woman who married the seventh son had powers over the weather, which strikes me as odd, but I wasn't there to refute it. I do know that every seventh son since then has had a power."

"What are some of the other powers the seventh sons have had?"

"Healing, moving through objects, very fast speed, being able to move somewhere in a single step, even if it's a mile away, control over animals, and so many more. Sometimes a power is repeated, and sometimes the youngest son will get a brand new power, like Fearghas. No one has ever seen this power of his, and it is a very strong gift. He's saved many lives with it."

"Yes, it seems to be a very good power." Caitlin pursed her lips. "What about the other brothers? Are they not jealous? I would think the eldest would be angry he's not getting to be laird."

Alana shook her head. "Nay, the others don't seem to mind at all. I think they're happy they don't get the burdens that go along with being laird. The powers are nice, but the responsibility is overwhelming."

The other women nodded.

"So now my job is to take care of the keep?" She wanted nothing to do with cleaning the huge castle, but she knew it was part of her responsibility.

"Yes, but only in that you'll be directing the maids and cooks. You can help on occasion, but it's not expected of you," Alana said with a smile.

"My brother and sister...where will they sleep?"

"Anywhere you want them to sleep. There is an empty room in the servants' quarters if you want to put them there, or there are seven empty chambers that my sons used when they were young. I would put them there, but the servant quarters are a good threat."

Caitlin smiled at that. "I need them close to keep an eye on them. They are used to running wild, while I take in sewing so we have money for food."

Alana sat down beside her on the sofa. "Trust me, there will be no more worries about money or food. All that will be taken care of. Your job will be directing the servants, and making sure your brother and sister are well-behaved."

Caitlin groaned. "I can oversee the servants, but Marta and Aileen? Have you met them?"

All of the women in the room chuckled at that. "Let Fearghas help you," Alana said softly. "He has powers that will help, as well as a good knowledge of how he and his brothers were punished when they misbehaved."

"I'll enlist his help. There is no doubt about that."

"Any more questions about our big secret?" Alana asked. "You can always ask later, of course, but I thought you may have more questions now."

Caitlin shook her head. "Nay. Nothing more now. There's enough for my mind to grapple with already."

Alana nodded, leaning forward to embrace Caitlin. "Welcome to our family."

For a moment, Caitlin forgot about the worries that had plagued her and simply enjoyed the embrace of a mother figure. It had been too long.

Chapter Three

After rejoining the feast, Caitlin spotted a few men carrying things out of the keep and others carrying things in. She didn't think she would have noticed it if she hadn't been watching for it. Obviously, even this was done in a way that made sense to everyone. They only did it once per generation, so she had no idea how everyone seemed so comfortable, but they obviously were.

Marta and Aileen walked to her when they returned from the cottage. "Did ye get everything?" Caitlin asked.

Aileen shrugged. "We put everything in the crates that the men brought us, and they carried it all off. It must be here."

"Thank you for seeing to the packing for me. I needed to be here."

Both of her siblings nodded. "Where will we sleep?" Marta asked.

"You'll be in the rooms the sons of the lair sleep in. They're all above stairs."

"We liked living with just you," Aileen said.

"And if you'd been able to behave and mind me, we'd still be living that way. But you were both caught misbehaving within minutes of each other. The laird's family had to step in."

Fearghas turned from a conversation he was having, pinning Aileen with a look. "Starting Monday, you'll be joining my young men in the army training. You won't have many choices for a good long while."

"I didn't mean to start a fire!"

"Oh, what were you doing then?"

Aileen frowned. "I was just playing in the woods with my friend."

"With your friend and everything you needed to make a fire...and then the fire itself. Nay. You'll be joining the young army

Marta frowned. "And what are you going to do with me?"

"You'll shadow your sister, learning everything you can from her. One of me cousins in Clan Campbell is in need of a wife. Perhaps I'll allow you to marry him if you behave well enough."

"Campbells? Everyone knows the Campbells are thieves." Marta protested.

"They're not thieves. They're family. Of course, since your sister didn't get to marry for love, neither do you. I'll make certain to find a man for you."

Marta was angry, and it was apparent on her face. "That's awful!"

Fearghas sighed. "I won't really force you into a marriage. Me mother was almost forced to marry, and she ran away from home. Nay, I won't force anything, but you must strive to be a good helper to your sister."

"Aye," Marta said, looking down.

"The two of ye will have the rooms all the way down the hall from us," he said. "Ye may go and look at them now."

They'd all lived in one room in the cottage, and having their own rooms should have been a wonderful thing to her siblings. Caitlin wasn't certain why they were being argumentative over this.

"Go," Caitlin echoed. The children needed to see them as united.

Both of them hurried toward the stairs to look at their new rooms. "I'm sorry they are so disobedient," Caitlin said.

Fearghas smiled, wrapping his arm around her shoulders and kissing her temple. "They'll be fine."

"I certainly hope so. I promised I'd care for them, but they don't want to be cared for. I'm their sister, not their mother."

"And I'm their laird. They'll listen to me."

"I hope so," Caitlin said. "We don't need a repeat of today."

"Nay, because then I'd have to convince you to marry me all over again."

The crowd in the keep seemed to have thinned a bit. She could see none of his brothers or sisters-in-law there except Murdoch and Lilli.

They had probably gone home to take care of the children and make sure they got to bed at a decent hour.

Murdoch and Lilli joined them and Caitlin sighed. "I guess you know all the family secrets now?" Caitlin asked Lilli."

Lilli shook her head, her eyes wide. "Nay. No one has told me a thing."

"'Tis my job to tell you later," Murdoch said, pulling her close and kissing her. "Brides aren't typically told the family secrets until they're members of the family."

Caitlin frowned. "I see."

"Tell me the secret!" Lilli said.

"You'll have to wait, lass," Murdoch grinned at her. "Just another hour or two. People are already starting for home."

Caitlin knew how Lilli hated secrets, and she wished she could tell her friend what was happening, but it just didn't work out that way. "It's not my secret to tell," Caitlin said softly to her friend. "I wish I could."

Lilli sighed. "I hate not knowing secrets."

Caitlin patted her friend's shoulder. "I know." She shook her head. "I wouldn't have mentioned it, but I thought you knew."

"I'd better know soon!" Lilli glared at Murdoch, and Caitlin laughed.

"I'm sure he'll tell you soon."

As the crowd grew thinner and thinner inside the keep, Alana walked up to the four of them who were still talking amongst themselves. "Caitlin, you should go up to the chamber at the top of the stairs and ready yourself for bed. Lilli? You do the same in your new cottage."

Lilli and Caitlin hugged. "We'll talk soon," Caitlin whispered to her friend.

"We will," Lilli agreed. "If not tomorrow, then I'll come by on Monday morning."

"That sounds good." Caitlin watched her friend leave before heading up the stairs of the keep. She had no pretty new nightgown to wear, and she was sad about that. She'd always known exactly the kind of nightgown she wanted for her wedding night, and now she wouldn't be able to have it.

To her surprise, Alana followed her into the bed chamber. "Long ago, I had my sister make nightgowns for all seven of my future daughters." She squatted down and pulled a trunk from under the bed. "This is the last one." She carefully put the white nightgown into Caitlin's hands. It had white lace around the neck, which is what Caitlin had planned to make.

"Oh, thank you, Lady McClain!"

"That name is yours now, not mine. Call me Alana."

Caitlin nodded. "Thank you, Alana."

"Get ready for bed, dear." Alana kissed Caitlin's cheek just before disappearing.

Caitlin quickly undressed and pulled the pretty nightgown over her head. It was perfect. She was unsure whether she would have a real wedding night, but she had a feeling Fearghas would insist.

She was waiting under the covers when he joined her in their bed chamber ten minutes later. She was surprised he'd given her that long. He walked into the room, blew out the single candle, and she heard sounds of him undressing in the dark.

Then the bed dipped, as he climbed in on the opposite side from her. "The feast lasted much longer than anyone expected."

"The clan received a new laird today. Of course, the feast was long."

"I suppose," he said softly. He tapped the spot beside him, and then had to move his hand over and over to finally find her, hugging the opposite side of the bed. "I don't bite."

She smiled. "I suppose I know that."

"Ye certainly should," he said. "Even my family wouldn't let a son be laird if he bit people."

She giggled. "I guess not."

"I know this wedding was sudden and not exactly what you wanted in life. I would understand if you wanted to wait for the wedding night."

"You would?" Surprised, she wasn't certain what she did want. "Perhaps we could get used to one another's touch, like an engaged couple would."

"I can do that. I may get a wee bit frustrated with touching you and not being able to make love, but that's to be expected."

"I dinna want to make you uncomfortable."

He laughed softly. "Too late, lass."

She moved to the middle of her side of the bed and quit clinging to the edge. "I do like your kisses."

"Well, that we can do." He cupped her face in his hands and kissed her, careful not to touch her anywhere else. Of course that was mostly for his benefit and not hers. He wasn't certain how he was going to be able to stop what he was doing already.

When he lifted his head after the kiss, he looked at her, barely able to see by the light of the quarter moon. "You're so beautiful."

She laughed softly. "You don't have to lie to me. I have done nothing special with my appearance since I took on the care of my siblings."

"I guess your beauty is all natural then. I do like it when you wear your hair down."

She smiled at that. "You've seen me with my hair down? When?"

"Early one morning, I was about to ride out of the village with some of me men, and I caught sight of you still in your nightgown. I promised myself then I'd be your husband someday."

"Why didn't you approach me then?"

He shrugged. "I did try. I asked Lilli to make certain the two of us could spend time with her and Murdoch. And she said she tried, but you wouldn't listen to her. So I tried at her wedding to me brother."

"So it's not just that I need help with me brother and sister? Or that I discovered your family secret?"

He smiled. "Those are the reasons the wedding was rushed. I'd have married you anyway."

"You think?" she asked. "I believe that my feelings for your family would have kept me from marrying you."

"It wouldn't have worked. I'd have spent all my time in your yard, begging for kisses, and my men would have gone untrained. It would have been terrible, but I'd have found a way."

"I see that you would have," Caitlin said, a slight smile on her lips. "I guess my brother and sister were just an excuse."

"A good one too, don't you think?"

She laughed. "I suppose it worked out the way you wanted."

"I know it did." He kissed her again, and this time, her arms went around him and explored his bare back, while his hands stroked down the sides of her neck and cupped her breasts.

When his lips followed the trail of one of his hands, she whispered, "That feels so good."

"'Tis meant to," he responded, one hand moving down to the juncture between her thighs. He stroked her there, and she arched against his touch. "Ye like that?"

"Yes, I do. What are you doing to me, Fearghas?"

"I like the sound of me name on your lips." His own lips captured one of her nipples and sucked it for a moment. "Are you sure we need to wait for the wedding night?"

"I'm sure it's a bad idea to wait," she told him. "Make love with me, Fearghas!"

His hand stayed between her thighs as he stroked her, trying to ready her for him. He kissed her and stroked her, and made her feel as if she was the woman most loved in all of Scotland.

When he covered her body with his and made them one, she couldn't believe she'd gone her whole life without doing this with a man. It felt too good to go for any period without doing it again. No wonder she would have seven children. She would be begging him to do this with her every night.

She gave herself over to the sensations, and her mind stopped working entirely. When she reached her climax, he moved more quickly within her until he ended it all with a shout.

As he moved to her side, she giggled. "I wonder if they heard us downstairs."

"I hope not. Though, I'm sure they would have all understood why I was having such a marvelous time."

"Hopefully my brother and sister are asleep and not listening for us to make noise."

"I completely forgot that the keep was full. All I could think about was how good it felt to be inside you. Well, I don't know that I was thinking at all to tell the truth."

"We'll have to do that often," she told him.

"Well, it is our job to provide seven sons for me parents to spoil."

"So if I have a daughter, it will be seven sons and one girl?"

"I'm sorry, lass. You won't get any daughters. There will be plenty of nieces and granddaughters, but you will have no daughters, unless you want to count Marta."

"That doesn't seem fair!"

"It worked out well for me mother because she only did wild boyish activities anyway. To this day, I don't think there's a man who can outshoot her in all the clan. Especially when she uses her pistol."

"What's a pistol?" Caitlin asked. She'd never heard of such a thing.

"Ask me mother tomorrow, and she'll show you. She carries one around her ankle, and the thing does a great deal more damage than an arrow. Someone from the future gave it to her."

Caitlin blinked a couple of times. "How does she know people from the future?"

"Three of my grandmothers are from the future," he said, grinning. "Me family is a great deal more unusual than you think."

"Oh, they couldn't be! I think they are the strangest people ever!"

He chuckled. "Fine. There's more to them than meets the eye."

"Well, I hope so. I know they have been the leaders of our clan for many years, but to me, they've just always seemed quite odd."

He shrugged. "Aye, clan leaders and good people through and through. There has not ever been a seventh son who didn't want good things for the world. I use my powers for good and not evil."

"What kind of evil could you use your powers for?" she asked.

He grinned. "I could use them to steal gold from other keeps. Just ride to the front, make a beckoning motion with my hand, and the money would come out to me. I tried it once with my older brother's sword, and though he was unhappy with me, it did work."

"I never thought of that. I suppose you enjoy using your powers?"

"Of course. I have something that no one else in the world has. No one to my knowledge anyway. I can do so many things with it, and I love every minute of it."

"So if you accidentally drop one of our sons off the balcony, you can wiggle your fingers and get him back?"

"I would prefer to never drop one of my children, but yes, I would be able to get them back if I saw it in time. But then my powers would be exposed to the entire clan, which would not be a good thing."

She snuggled closer to him. "As long as my child survives, nothing else really matters."

Fearghas chuckled, and wrapped his arms around her. "Goodnight, Caitlin."

"Goodnight, Fearghas."

His heart flipped every time she said his name. Life could not get better than it was at that moment.

Chapter Four

The following day was Sunday and a lazy day around the keep. Caitlin woke earlier than she'd thought she would after the festivities of the previous day. She ventured downstairs to the kitchen, and Cook told her she would have breakfast ready in a few minutes.

"Have you seen my brother or sister yet?" Caitlin asked.

Cook shook her head. "Nay, but I'll cook for them when they're ready."

"They've already slept much later than usual. I'll go wake them now." Caitlin hurried back up the stairs to find Marta and Aileen. They were both still sleeping. "Up you get!" she told them. "We're going to have to have some rules, and one of those is not sleeping late."

Marta lifted her head from her pillow. "Are you still angry?"

Caitlin considered the question for a moment before shaking her head. "Nay, I'm not angry, but I will not allow you to act the way you have been. Get up, breakfast is almost ready."

When she saw that both of them were getting up, she went down the hall to the chamber she shared with Fearghas. "Cook will have breakfast done in a few minutes."

He caught her wrist and pulled her into bed on top of him. "I have an idea for what to do for those few minutes," he said, kissing her.

She laughed, pushing away. "My brother and sister are on their way down. I came into this marriage with children, even if I didn't give birth to them."

He sighed. "Yes, and today we start giving them structure. Get off me, woman! I need to get dressed."

Caitlin shook her head. "Are you always this insane in the mornings?"

He thought about it for a moment before shaking his head. "No, but I don't usually have a faerie in my chamber before I've broken my fast." He rolled to the side of the bed and sat up, ignoring his own nudity. "Next time tell me what is happening before you attack me in bed."

She put her hands on her hips. "I refuse to listen to your nonsense. I shall see you at breakfast." With that, she opened the door just enough to leave and shut it behind her.

She hurried down the stairs and popped her head into the kitchen again. "Fearghas, as well as my brother and sister, will be joining me for breakfast."

Cook frowned. "Mayhap you should leave your brother and sister with me, while you and Fearghas find some alone time."

"We have much to say to the children, so that will not work."

"'Tis a pity," Cook said, turning her attention back to the eggs she was cooking. "I'll bring tortillas in with the eggs and bacon, and then you can make breakfast burritos if you'd like."

Since she'd come to the village, Caitlin had learned about both flour and corn tortillas, but she'd never heard of a breakfast burrito. "How can we make them?"

Cook laughed. "Fearghas will show you. Breakfast burritos are his favorite breakfast."

"I will enjoy learning," Caitlin said. "Is there anything I can do to help?"

"Nay. 'Tis not your place to help in the kitchen. You eat with your family."

Caitlin went back out to the dining room and saw everyone had gathered there already. Fearghas was clothed now, but he looked particularly tired. "It shall be ready in a minute. Fearghas, you must teach us to make breakfast burritos."

He grinned. "I love breakfast burritos."

"Then you'll show us?"

He nodded. "Of course."

When the food was brought out, Fearghas immediately picked up a tortilla, and added eggs, bacon, and a small bit of cheese. "It's that simple."

"So it's like a taco with eggs and bacon instead of mincemeat?"

"Basically," he said.

The others followed suit and they all had the new food for their breakfast. "I never had corn before moving to the village. Or tomatoes. And certainly not tacos," Caitlin said.

"They're New World foods," he said. "Our clan has had them for many generations, but only because some of my grandmothers traveled back in time and had the forethought to bring seeds. They claimed to be incapable of living without tacos."

Caitlin shook her head. "This is the second time you've told me some of your grandmothers traveled back in time. How do you expect me to take you seriously when you say things like this?"

"I'll show you proof after we've eaten," he said casually.

Her brother and sister were quietly eating their burritos, and she had a feeling they were trying to escape their notice. "I think Fearghas had a bit too much of the grape last night. Don't you?"

Marta laughed softly. "If he keeps talking about traveling through time, then yes, much too much grape."

Fearghas frowned as the three siblings laughed. "I'll have you know, I'm telling the truth!" He looked at Marta. "Can you read?"

Marta shook her head. "Nay. I never learned."

Then he looked at Aileen. "Can you read?"

He shook his head. "Why do I need to read? I'm to be a soldier!"

Fearghas shrugged. "My mother believes everyone should be able to read."

"I would like to learn," Caitlin said. "Perhaps you can teach me?"

"Most likely my mother will teach you. And provide you with many books to read." Fearghas spoke as if he knew all about reading and how his mother would handle things.

"I would like that," she said. "And I know my brother and sister should learn to read as well."

Fearghas nodded before looking at Aileen. "You may learn in the mornings, and in the afternoon, you will train."

Aileen frowned. "But I don't want to learn to read."

"You're not being given a choice in the matter," Fearghas said. "You've shown that when you do have a choice, you never do the right thing. Going forward, that is going to change."

Aileen nodded. "Yes, laird."

As soon as they'd finished breakfast, Fearghas suggested the four of them walk around the loch and talk. Caitlin knew he was going to talk about the rules they would have in their family, and she hoped her siblings gave him the respect due the laird, and not just the brother.

"You'll both wake in the morning and have breakfast with your sister and me as a family," he said. "Then you will learn from whoever is assigned to teach you to read. All three of you will learn together."

Caitlin nodded. She was so excited to learn.

"Then after learning, we will have the noon meal together, and then Caitlin and Marta will spend the afternoon together, learning how to manage a house as large as the keep, and Aileen will report to the younger men's training grounds. There will be no excuses for missing training."

Caitlin frowned. "That sounds harsh. What if Aileen is sick?"

"Then you will send someone for a healer. My grandfather is a healer as well as my great uncle. It would take but moments for most maladies to be healed."

"Is that their power?" she asked.

He nodded. "You will soon be used to the odd ways of my family."

"I hope so," she said. For a moment she started to bring up the woman who had glared at her all day the previous day, but she knew that she didn't want to discuss it in front of her brother and sister.

"Do any of you have questions for me?" Fearghas asked.

"What about when training is done for the day?" Aileen asked. "May I spend time with my friends then?"

"After you've reported to your sister and gotten her permission. She will let you know what you can and cannot do. Now, let's talk about punishments for disobeying her. Aileen, the first time you disobey, you will be given to the stablemaster, to do whatever jobs he sees fit. You will work after training all day and on Sunday if he deems it necessary for you to be forgiven your disobedience. Marta, if you disobey, your sister will assign you tasks to make up for what you've done. If you disobey again, you will report to me. I will find a worse task for you to accomplish. Is that understood?"

The children answered together. "Aye."

"For the remainder of today, you may make your rooms to your liking."

"Rooms?" Marta asked. "We shared one last night."

Fearghas shook his head. "You will each have your own room."

Marta looked excited. "I've always wanted my own room."

"And ye shall have it. Any questions?"

Both shook their heads and ran for the keep, obviously excited about what they would do to their room. "We all shared a room in the cottage," Caitlin said softly. "There was no question of who got their own because there were no more rooms to give."

"Why didn't you bring your troubles to the laird when you were having so much trouble? I know Father would have helped!"

"I thought it was my problem. The laird wasn't asked by my mother on her death bed to care for my brother and sister. I was."

"But your life could have been much easier. I believe Father would have simply moved all three of you into the keep. Of course, then I wouldn't have been able to keep my hands off of you, and I'd have spent more time in your bed chamber than my own..."

She shook her head. "My parents would have rolled over in their graves. Nay, it was my job to care for them, and I did my very best."

"Now you can share the difficulty with me." He took her hand in his as he kept up his slow walk around the loch.

"There was a woman at the feast yesterday. She was glaring at me, as if I'd done something wrong to her. I'd never seen her before. Do you know who it could be?"

He shook his head. "What did she look like? I haven't been courting another lass if that's what you're asking."

"She had blond hair. Slim. I couldn't see the color of her eyes, but they were constantly narrowed and pointed in my direction. As I don't know her, I thought mayhap you did."

"I don't think so. I can't imagine anyone who would be upset with the two of us marrying."

"Just keep thinking on it. If I see her again, I'll be certain to point her out to you."

"Were you afraid for any reason?" he asked.

"Not afraid, but I was uncomfortable with the look she kept giving me."

"I'll ask my family if anyone noticed her. And we'll continue to watch for her," Fearghas said, not willing to write off any potential danger to his bride.

"Thank you," she said softly.

He stopped walking and took her into his arms. "You're my wife and the mother of my seven unborn sons."

"What if I only give birth to two sons?"

He chuckled. "I've been told each new bride asks the same thing. And each one then gives birth to seven sons, the youngest wielding a power of some sort. Just as you will." He leaned down and pressed his lips to hers. "If only we could get away with a nap..."

She laughed. "My brother and sister are too old to believe we're taking naps in the middle of the day."

"I should have married you years ago!"

"When I was a child myself? I'm not certain that would have been smart."

"How old were you when your parents were taken from you?"

"I was fourteen summers. I'm eighteen summers now."

"Perhaps I married you at just the right time. We'll have to send your siblings on many errands."

She laughed. "I wouldn't argue too much with that."

"We must walk to my mother's house and let her know she'll have three to teach to read on the morrow."

"Will she mind?"

"If she does, she'll assign a grandmother or one of my aunts. She made sure everyone knew how to read."

"And what is there for all of these people to read?" Caitlin asked. "I've never seen a real book."

"Come, let's go see my mother, and she will show you."

Caitlin didn't ask more questions as she walked alongside Fearghas to her old cottage, which was now inhabited by his parents. He knocked loudly on the door. His mother came to see who it was. "Why were ye tryin' ta break me door down?"

"Sorry," Fearghas said, but the grin on his face belied his words. "Caitlin needs proof that people came from the future, and she and her siblings need to get reading lessons every morning for a while."

Alana smiled. "I remember when your grandmother taught me to read." She opened the door wider. "Come in, and I'll give you proof."

Caitlin stepped inside, wondering if there was actually anything that would convince her that people had come from the future. Alana picked up a rectangular object that was completely smooth. She pushed a button, and the whole thing lit up. "This is called an iPad. It comes from the twenty-first century." With a few taps of her finger, she showed her a long series of paintings with words on them. "These are books. All written in the future about our time. 'Tis funny to read them because you discover that what they thought was truth about our time was utter gibberish."

Caitlin smiled, running her fingers over the thing. "This came from the future?"

Alana nodded. "It has many books, but it also has games. My sons all played with things like these as children."

"My favorite was Angry Birds," Fearghas said. "There was a giant slingshot, and I would shoot birds at pigs. I played it often."

"That sounds very strange," Caitlin said.

"My favorite was a game called Candy Crush. You had to match different colored pieces of candy and they would be crushed. My mother-in-law liked to tell me that the candy didn't crush itself if she wasn't there to do it. I always giggled."

"So you spent your entire marriage playing games and reading books on this thing?"

"Much of it. I read to my boys from it, and I taught them to read from it. I do love reading."

"I'm excited to learn myself," Caitlin said softly.

"Do ye believe in the women who came back in time then?" Fearghas asked.

"It still seems like a tale told to small children to me. I don't think I do believe it."

Alana smiled. "You will. I promise you. After tomorrow, you will."

Chapter Five

Back at the keep, Caitlin checked in on her brother and sister. Marta and Aileen were separating their belongings and carrying them into their own rooms. Outside the room they'd shared the night before, they'd placed a pile of Caitlin's things.

Caitlin immediately picked up the things they'd marked as hers and carried them down the hall to the chamber she shared with Fearghas. When Fearghas spotted her carrying her own things he frowned. "You should ask one of the servants to do that. It's not your job."

Caitlin shrugged. "They're my things, and that makes it my job." Surely he could see the logic behind that.

"You're going to be a stubborn wife, aren't you?" Fearghas asked, shaking his head at her.

"I won't ask others to do work I'm perfectly capable of doing if that's what you mean," she said. "Why would I?"

"Because you're not meant to do that kind of work anymore. You're the laird's wife."

She nodded. "And as the laird, you let someone else train your men and don't do any real work yourself?"

"I have to train my men. It's my job."

"And this is mine," she said softly, as she looked around the room for a place to put her belongings. "May I use one of these trunks?"

"Aye. Me mother emptied them yesterday, so they're yours to do with as you see fit."

"Thank ye!" She pulled the trunk his mother had gotten her nightgown from away from the wall. When she opened it, she paused, looking at the contents. It was full of clothing for babies. She wouldn't need to sew for her sons for a good long while it seemed. "Will she want these baby clothes? Or are they for our sons."

He walked over and looked in the trunk. "I believe they were the clothes my brothers and I wore as babies. Mother would have left them here for our sons."

"Do you think she left clothes for when the boys are older?"

He laughed. "We destroyed everything we touched. I'm sure there are no clothes from when we were older."

"That makes sense. There's not much a baby can do to ruin what they wear." She decided that she would sew clothes for toddlers and children, but not for babies. There was obviously enough for when the boys were small.

While Caitlin finished her task, Fearghas went through the other trunks in the room, making sure they were empty. And it seemed most were, with the exception of the one Caitlin had found, and another that was filled with children's books.

Fearghas held up one of the books and smiled. "This was my favorite book when I was a little boy."

Caitlin looked at him to see him holding up a photo of a blue furry thing. "What is it called?" she asked.

"The Monster at the End of This Book. It's about this blue thing here, who is afraid all through the book because there is a monster at the end, but it turns out he's the monster he was so afraid of. I must have read it a hundred times."

"Did your brothers enjoy it as well?" Caitlin asked.

He shrugged. "They were enough older that if they did like it, they wouldn't have admitted it to me. I don't mind though. Sometimes it's nice to remember things you liked when you were a boy."

She nodded. "I had a doll. She was just cloth, but I remember her being my prized possession."

"Do you still have her?" Fearghas asked.

"No, I passed her on to Marta a very long time ago, and she ended up tearing her up. She was not as gentle with her things as I was."

He nodded. "That sounds like how it was in our family. Everything was ruined by the time it was my turn to play with it." He still remembered yearly visits from a woman with purple hair who came from the future. She brought him toys. He wasn't about to bring that up to Caitlin though because she would just argue with him. Soon, she'd believe him.

"What was your favorite toy?" she asked.

"It was a little horseless carriage," he responded.

She laughed. "How did it get anywhere then?"

"I pushed it of course." There had been many toys that had come from the future, but his favorite was a red car. He knew his mother still had it somewhere for his children to play with. He simply didn't know where.

She grinned, shaking her head as she continued packing things into the trunks there. Once they had everything put away, she walked downstairs to see what Cook was making for lunch, already feeling hungry.

Cook smiled when she stuck her head into the kitchen. "Are ye hungry?"

Caitlin nodded emphatically. "Very."

"I'm making a stew for lunch, and I thought I'd make baked potatoes with cheese and bacon for supper."

"That all sounds wonderful," she said. "How long until lunch?"

"It's ready. Just let me know when you want me to serve it."

"Fifteen minutes?"

"Sounds good," Cook responded.

Caitlin went back upstairs to let Fearghas, Marta and Aileen know their lunch plans. Her brother and sister were used to just having a bit of bread and milk for their noon meal, so they were excited to know they would have a real meal.

As they ate, Aileen talked about how excited he was to have a room of his own. "I canna believe I get to have a room with no girls in it. No one can touch my things, and no one to bother me. I can even sleep without hearing my sisters snore."

Caitlin rolled her eyes. "We don't snore." She looked over at Marta. "How is your room?"

"It's so big for just one person. I feel almost ashamed to not be sharing it. But it is nice to know I can get up when I want and go to sleep when I want, and I don't have to worry about waking anyone." Marta looked positively gleeful.

"This afternoon, I think we should all do something together," Fearghas said. He looked at Marta. "Do you ride?"

She shook her head. "Nay."

Caitlin smiled. "I rode a little when I was younger, but after mother had these two, it became harder to find the time to get away."

"I don't ride either," Aileen said. "Pa was supposed to teach me."

"How long ago did your parents die?" Fearghas asked.

"Four years ago. I was only fourteen years old when I took on the raising of Marta and Aileen. It was harder than I want to admit."

"It's hard to respect a sister in the same way you do your parents," Aileen said. "I think that's why we disobeyed so often."

"But those days are behind us now, right?" Fearghas asked.

Both of them nodded. "No boy will have anything to do with me now that I'm related to the laird," Marta said sadly.

Caitlin shook her head. "You need to wait until you're older," she said. "You shouldn't be courting if you're not old enough to marry, and despite what you think, you're not old enough to marry."

"Other girls marry at thirteen!" Marta argued.

Fearghas nodded. "And by law, girls can marry at twelve, but you are too young to marry. And now, as your sister has married me, you must get my approval to marry."

Marta sighed. "My life is over."

"I think it may be time for you to move to Edenborough and become an actress. This keep isn't big enough for all your drama," Caitlin said.

Marta made a face, but she continued eating her stew.

Aileen laughed at his sister. "Your life may be over, but mine is better now. I don't have to be the man of the family anymore, and I get the respect that comes with being a member of the laird's family."

Fearghas shut that line of thinking down quickly. "Instead of thinking of yourself as a member of my family, think of it as if you're a member of my junior army. You're not even ranked high enough to become a soldier."

Aileen sighed, deflating completely, his shoulders sagging. "You could let me dream for a day or two."

"Are you or are you not the boy who tried to set my woods on fire yesterday?"

"You put it out easily."

"Aye, I did. Or the keep and the entire village would have burned down. You deserve no elevating of your status." Though the fire had been small, Fearghas wanted to impress upon the boy that his shenanigans could end in disaster.

"Aye, Laird." Aileen stared down at his bowl for a moment before mopping up the stew with his bread.

"We'll go for a walk this afternoon, as neither of you know how to ride a horse. That will change soon, but not today. Today, we will walk and talk, and get to know one another better."

Caitlin smiled. "That sounds like fun to me."

"Not to me," Marta complained. "I want to see Calum. I haven't gotten to see him since you scared us in the woods yesterday."

Fearghas frowned. "Yes, of course you may see him. I'll walk you over there after our meal, and you can explain to his parents what the two of you were doing in the woods while you were supposed to be at me brother's wedding feast."

Aileen snorted at Fearghas's response. "I have a feeling he's out of your life for good!"

"And young Donald and his mother deserve a visit as well, don't ye think?" Donald was the boy who had been with Aileen in the woods the previous day.

Aileen frowned. "Nay, laird. I'll walk with you happily."

When Fearghas glanced at Caitlin, he was certain she'd be annoyed by the way he was talking to her brother and sister, but instead, she had a smile on her face that went from ear to ear. Obviously, she was pleased with him, and he was glad. It would be hard enough to fight the children. He shouldn't have to fight Caitlin as well.

When they started out on their walk, they saw Calum, and when he slowed down, looking to talk to Marta, she turned her face away. Caitlin smiled. "Mayhap she's learning," she whispered to Fearghas.

"It's time for her to learn," he whispered back. They walked toward the Campbell land. "One of my grandmothers was a Campbell."

Marta turned to him. "But I thought all Campbells were murderers and thieves."

"Nay," Fearghas replied. "They are good people. We still consider them to be our sister clan. My grandfather married one of the laird's daughters."

Caitlin nodded her understanding. It wasn't as if two random people of the two clans had married. It was a laird's son to a laird's daughter. That was much different. "We are sister clans after that."

When they crossed onto Campbell land, no one seemed to think anything of it. The guards posted on the other land, waved a hand for them to go on. There was a road that would take them to the village near the Campbells' keep, but Fearghas didn't head that way. Instead, he was trying to see what the two children he now had a responsibility for were worth.

He thought a great deal of their sister, but he would send Aileen away to be fostered if it came to that. He couldn't risk having too much happening in his own household for him to be able to see to his duties as laird.

When they spotted a stag, Fearghas looked at Aileen. "Can you kill it for our supper?"

Aileen shook his head, looking embarrassed. "Nay. I have never shot an arrow."

Fearghas nodded. "Then you should learn. By the time my mother married, she could outshoot all the men in our clan," he said, grinning.

"I've heard it said that men marry women who are like their mothers. That is not the case here. I have never been one to touch a weapon, let alone use one," Caitlin told him.

"I'll teach you," he said, not really giving her the option. He wanted her to be able to protect herself if he wasn't beside her. "And you, Marta."

"I don't need to learn to shoot," Marta scoffed. "I'll always have a man by my side who will take care of any animals or scoundrels for me."

Fearghas frowned. "Many women think that. You will learn to shoot. I will not leave you unprotected if the unspeakable were to occur."

Marta shrugged. "I suppose I have no say in the matter."

"Not in this you don't," Fearghas replied.

"You don't even carry a bow! You couldn't protect us if something were to happen!"

"I don't need to. I can fight off animals and men alike with my bare hands."

Aileen said, "I've heard that about you. What would you do if that stag charged us?"

"I would kill it, and then we'd all be carrying meat home to have it for our supper."

"But how?"

"With my hands," Fearghas said.

"You can't kill an animal that big with your hands," Marta said.

"He killed an adder right before I stepped on it yesterday," Caitlin said softly. "He saved my life. I had no weapon, and he didn't either. I could have died."

Marta narrowed her eyes. "How did you kill an adder with no weapon?"

"With my hands," Fearghas said simply. He turned then and took another path toward the woods they shared with the Campbell Clan.

"Do you even know where you're going?" Aileen asked.

Caitlin was mortified at the question. Her younger siblings needed to start showing respect to Fearghas.

"Aye, I know where we're going. This path will take us into the woods, and I'll show you the area you burned yesterday."

Aileen sighed. "Will I never hear the end of that?"

"Have you done anything to repair the damage you did?" Fearghas asked. "You killed an area of land. I know you killed at least one tree. You must go and chop down that tree so another can grow in its place. For you to destroy part of our woods with your foolhardiness is unacceptable."

"I'll work on that the first chance I get, but it does sound like you have my days planned out for a while."

"Next Sunday, when everyone else is taking their rest day, you and I will go and I will show you the proper way to chop down a tree."

"Yes, Laird," Aileen said, and the annoyance was clear in his voice.

Caitlin was amazed that Fearghas had kept his temper with them for as long as he had. He was a good man. The more time he spent with her and her siblings, the more she could see it.

Chapter Six

The following morning, after they'd had breakfast together, Alana and several older women walked into the keep. "Are you ready to learn to read?" Alana asked.

Caitlin bit her lip and nodded. She worried she wouldn't be able to learn. It seemed to her that only the smartest people around were able to read. She wouldn't voice her worries, though because she didn't want her brother and sister to feel any of the uneasiness she was experiencing.

Fearghas kissed her goodbye to go train his men, leaving her with many older women. "I thought we could first introduce ourselves, as I'm certain you don't know all of us," Alana said. "I'm Alana, and you already know I'm Fearghas's mother."

"I'm Brynna, Fearghas's grandmother."

"I'm Holli, Fearghas's great-grandmother, and I'm from the future." The older woman had a smile on her face, and Caitlin found she couldn't even meet her eyes. This made no sense.

"I'm Heather, Fearghas's great-great grandmother, and I'm from the future as well."

"I'm Beth, Fearghas's great-great-great grandmother, from the future."

Caitlin had no idea what to say to that. "Do people from the future live so much longer than we do?"

Beth was the one to answer. "Yes, but even more than that, with the ability to heal coming up often, we've never gotten sick enough to die. So we keep on going. My husband, Gavin, has the healing touch, and he refuses to die until there's no more threat of plague at all. Even though he has grandsons who could easily take care of anyone who became ill."

"As someone who lost her parents to the plague, I'm glad they are still ready for whatever comes." Caitlin didn't have to believe the women came from the future to say kind things.

Alana stood up. "I think it's going to go better if all of you learn to read one on one. So I will teach my new daughter-in-law."

Brynna smiled. "I'll teach Marta. And I want to hear all about what happened in the woods with Calum. I've heard many rumors."

"And I'll teach Aileen," Holli said. "Maybe I can get him to show me where he started the fire with Donald."

Caitlin noticed her siblings both had the good manners to look embarrassed to have their misdeeds talked about. Good. She knew it would be best if they realized people were watching them and all they did.

Alana and Caitlin went upstairs to work together. Caitlin noticed her mother-in-law was carrying the thing they'd called an iPad the day before. "I hope you don't mind if I use this to teach you. I know it's from the future, but it's what I was taught to read on as well."

"You couldn't read when you married into the family?" Caitlin asked, thrilled to not feel quite so alone.

Alana shook her head. "Nay. I trained with me father's men and did nothing inside. My sister could manage a household, but even she hadn't been taught to read and write."

"Fearghas said when you married, you could outshoot every McClain soldier."

Alana laughed. "'Tis true. And then someone from the future brought me this." Alana leaned down and took something from a little belt she wore around her ankle.

"What is it?" Caitlin asked.

"It's called a pistol." Alana held it up. "It uses gunpowder, which is the same thing used to shoot off cannons. I myself have never seen a cannon, but I understand they are often used in warfare. Anyway, I aim at whatever I need to aim at, shoot, and these little metal things called bullets are shot at whatever I aim at. The bullets do more damage than an arrow. I prefer not to use it, but I will if necessary."

"You only have one?" Caitlin thought it would be easier to learn to shoot than a bow and arrow.

Alana nodded. "Yes, only one. It's one of those future things that most of the clan don't know about. Like the iPads." Alana put her pistol back where it had been and put the iPad on her lap. "This has a battery which holds the power to run the thing. We charge it with the sun." She pushed a button on the top of the device, and a painting showed immediately.

"How did you do that?"

Alana laughed. "I couldn't explain how it worked. I just know what to do to make it go." She tapped something on the screen and then held it up between her and Caitlin. There was a bright flash, and then Alana showed Caitlin what she'd done. "That's called a photograph. That's how you look right now."

"What is this magic?"

"It's future technology. That's about all I know about it."

"It is interesting." Caitlin wanted to take it and flip it over and see how it worked, but she knew she was supposed to be learning to read.

"All right. Today, I'm going to teach you to recognize the letters. It should be easy."

So together they worked until they were called for lunch. When Caitlin descended the stairs, she realized Beth and Heather had gone home, but the other women seemed to be eating with them.

Fearghas came in and joined them, and they all gathered around the dining table. "Believe me now?"

"I don't want to, but I can't seem to stop myself."

He smiled, putting his arm around her. "You'll get used to our ways soon enough."

"I'm not sure that's possible," Caitlin said, shaking her head.

He laughed softly. "Are all of you staying for lunch?" he asked the three women who were part of his patriarchal line.

"Yes, if we're teaching, then you're feeding us," Holli said with a smile.

"Sounds good to me."

The lunch was a simple soup, but it was filling, and that was all that really mattered. As they ate, Alana said, "I'll be staying after lunch to show you and Marta how to run a household."

Caitlin nodded. "I'd like that." Sure, she knew how to manage a three-person household in the village, but she had no idea how to run a household as big as the keep, which she was told was added to with each new generation. In the main part of the keep, where she lived, there were eight bedrooms, the great hall, the parlor, kitchen, and dining room. But she knew there were both east and west wings that had been added on for when the clan was hosting a great event.

"And you'll report to the junior soldiers after we eat," Fearghas told Aileen. "You'll be the youngest soldier there, which means everyone gets to boss you around. I'm sure you'll enjoy it."

Aileen groaned. "It's bad enough I have to learn to read."

"And you'll learn to be a man by training with the soldiers. You don't think your sister can teach you that, do you?"

After lunch, while Brynna and Holli went to their respective homes, Alana explained how to plan meals and work with the cook on them. "We have maids who clean the keep, but I always tried to at least do the dusting in my chamber and the parlor, as those are the rooms I use most. Someone else will come along and sweep and scrub the floors, and you may find you want to do more around the keep than those things, but I kept up my training after I married."

"I see," Caitlin said. "The principles you're teaching us? Can they be used for a smaller house as well?"

"Oh, aye. You're both learning what you'll need to know to be good wives."

Caitlin realized she hadn't taught Marta as much as she should have. That day, they darned stockings, and there were so many to darn, Marta finally threw the stockings into the basket where they were kept.

"He's not my husband. I don't have to mend his stockings!"

Caitlin opened her mouth, but she found her mother-in-law was already responding. "So you don't think you should have to do anything to earn your keep?"

Marta gaped at her. "I…"

"You will work with your sister, and you will be thankful that you have a roof over your head. Your sister has been working for years to keep you and your brother warm and fed. And this is how you repay her? By telling her you shouldn't have to mend her husband's stockings? And who, pray tell, has mended your stockings since your parents died? Who has made all your meals? You should be on your knees kissing your sister's feet, not complaining you are expected to do a couple hours of light work. I'm absolutely disgusted with you, Marta." Alana reached into the basket and threw several socks at Marta, making sure each hit her in the face. "Now get to work."

"Aye, Lady McClain," Marta said, lowering her head to look at the stockings.

Caitlin started to say something when she saw the glint of tears in her sister's eyes, but Alana put her hand on her arm and shook her head. "I've heard wonderful things about your talent with a needle and thread," Alana said to Caitlin.

"Thank you. I mainly mended things for men who were unmarried, or women who were too busy to do their own mending. It's how I kept food on the table."

"Doesn't sewing for long hours make your head ache?" Alana asked.

Caitlin nodded. "It does. It's been nice the past couple of days because the headache is gone, and the spot between my shoulders doesn't ache nearly so much."

"But it still hurts?" Alana asked.

"I'm not sure the ache will ever leave me."

"Let me talk to Holli about it. She was something called a massage therapist before she came back in time. She can rub the pain right out of you."

"I wouldn't ask her to do that!"

Alana smiled. "I'll make sure she's healed before and after. But her hands can work miracles. You'll need to see her often while you're expecting. I did."

"I couldn't ask someone her age to work so hard."

"Trust me, she'll be thrilled to do it. She misses her old life sometimes. I think if she hadn't been sent back in time with her two best friends, it would have been much harder for her. They still get together almost every day, even if only to have a picnic by the loch."

"Picnic?" Caitlin asked. It wasn't a word she knew.

"I forget that's a word that we learned from them. A picnic is a lunch or light meal outdoors. Usually on a blanket."

"I've had many picnics then. I just didn't know they were called that."

Alana grinned. "Well, they're not yet. But they will be!"

Caitlin laughed. "I don't know how you keep all these things straight."

"It becomes easier. I didn't feel as if I really belonged here until my sister also left Clan McKay and joined me here. You'll find your siblings to be joys once they learn to obey."

Marta looked like she was going to say something to that, but she stayed silent, which was fine with Caitlin. Her sister tended to anger her more often than not.

Finally, at the end of the day, Alana put the stockings she hadn't yet finished into the basket and nodded to the large pile they had finished. "I think that was a good day's work."

Caitlin nodded. "I certainly couldn't have done all of that on my own."

"You'll find that we'll discuss many things as we darn those stockings, and you'll learn much that way." Alana stood. "I'll be back in the morning to give you another reading lesson."

"Thank you for taking so much time to help me. You should be enjoying these years of rest now though."

"No, I always knew it was my job to train you as Brynna trained me. I'll have plenty of years to do nothing but hunt."

Caitlin laughed. "Mayhap I could learn to hunt from you as well."

"Oh, no," Alana said, shaking her head. "I cannot teach anyone to hunt. I've tried, but I get too impatient. I think everyone should be able to pick up a bow and arrow and hit a target. I'm not the person for that."

"That's all right," Caitlin said. "Fearghas has offered."

"That is a much better idea," Alana said, heading for the door. "We'll learn the sounds of the letters tomorrow."

After she was gone, Caitlin looked at her sister. "Are you better now?"

"Why did you let her talk to me that way?" Marta asked. "I'm your sister!"

"You are. But she's my mother-in-law, and she's right. I did too much to make sure you and Aileen had it easier than you should have. I spoiled you both because you'd lost your mother and father. It didn't matter that I'd lost mine too."

"But you enjoy sewing! You told me."

"I enjoy it when I'm doing it to make something I want. I don't enjoy sewing when I'm doing everyone else's mending. But you survived because I was willing to take in sewing."

Marta looked like she wasn't sure if she should be angry or sad. "I should have done more to help."

"Aye, you should have. And Aileen should have as well. But I didn't force you, and now you don't respect me. That needs to change. If

Fearghas had seen you throw the stockings back into the basket, you'd be punished. I won't say anything, but you need to show more respect."

Marta nodded, but she still looked like she was upset by the entire conversation.

When Aileen and Fearghas came in at the end of the day, Aileen looked as if he could barely walk. "Were you injured?" Caitlin asked, worried about her brother.

"He spent the day moving rocks from one pile to another. 'Tis how the young soldiers get stronger. He aches now, but he'll be thankful for it later."

Aileen stood straight and glared at Fearghas. "I will never be thankful for the way you treat me."

Fearghas nodded. "All right. But you will not speak to me in the tone you're using."

"Aye, Laird," Aileen said, walking toward the stairs.

"Supper will be ready in just a few minutes," Caitlin said. "I would wait before going up." She could see by her brother's movements that once he made it upstairs, he wouldn't be coming down again that night.

"I want my supper in my bed," Aileen said.

"Nay," Fearghas responded. "You already have an easier life than the other young soldiers because you are living here in the keep and not in the barracks, where the boys take turns cooking. If you want to go up now, you will have no supper."

Aileen glared at Fearghas, but nodded. Caitlin realized then just how spoiled her brother and sister were. Never would she have realized until she saw how they reacted to Fearghas. They would need to learn manners quickly to avoid his ire.

Chapter Seven

By the following Sunday, Caitlin could read simple books. It felt like a major victory to her. Her siblings were still unhappy with their new situations, but they were doing as they were told, and that pleased her more than she could express.

Caitlin had finally realized that the odd family she'd feared for so long was filled with wonderful people, many of whom could teach her a great deal. Instead of worrying about them, she rejoiced to be among them. And Fearghas continued to make her happy, both in bed and out. He was a good man to have on her side.

On Sunday afternoon, they had a picnic out by the loch, and it felt incredibly romantic to Caitlin. Her brother and sister were along, but they were wandering around the lake on their own instead of staying with Caitlin and Fearghas, who they were still angry with.

Fearghas popped a small bite of food into her mouth, and she smiled, kissing his fingers. "Thank ye for insisting that we marry. I find myself much happier than I was alone. It's nice to be able to share my burden with someone." And to her surprise, laird business hadn't kept him from his family.

He smiled. "I will always help you with your burdens. Despite his constant arguing, Aileen has done well with the other young men training to be soldiers. He seems to be making friends with my nephew, Kevin, which is good because Kevin will keep him in line."

"I wondered how that was going, but I was truly afraid to ask. I worried the other boys wouldn't understand him the same way I do."

"I think he's realizing that being an orphan doesn't give him an excuse for bad behavior. When he's a man it won't matter what happened in his childhood. He will need to be strong and willing to do all he can for his clan regardless."

Caitlin nodded. "I never should have coddled the two of them the way I did after our parents died. I felt as if we all grieved together, we could all grow together, but instead, they grew into monsters."

"We're settling all that. Right now, they think of me as the enemy, and though they're angry with you for marrying me, they know they must obey. Soon, things will be a great deal easier than they have been."

"I can read short, easy books now."

"That's wonderful!" he said. "Do you enjoy reading?"

She nodded. "It's like there was a secret code surrounding me my entire life that I couldn't seem to understand. Now that I've been given the key, it's opening up so much for me."

"My favorite thing when I was a little boy was my mother reading to me. I didn't want my children to miss out on that special experience."

"That sounds lovely. I'll keep working on my reading until I'm certain I can read to them. I really want to spend some time learning things like history. Your mother told me the whole world was on that iPad thing, and I'd love to learn all about it."

"One of the iPads has history books on it. They all have Highland romance novels, which I find strange, but I can't question my great grandmothers about it. One is all about science. They were careful to be certain they would have what they need technologically when they came back in time."

"So it's just the three of them who came back?" she asked. "Heather, Holli, and Beth?"

He smiled, shaking his head. "Nay, Alyssa as well. But she married one of my father's uncles, and so she's not in the main family line. She still spends time with her two best friends Heather and Holli though."

"I'm never going to keep your family members straight," she said. "I thought I was doing well, but I'm not."

"That's fine. I have a huge family, and I can't expect you to learn them all."

"I appreciate you learning the names of my brother and sister, even though I've never attempted to do the same."

"There are only three of you. Much easier to learn."

As they watched, the boy who had started the fire with Aileen the previous week came out of the woods and began to walk with Aileen and Marta. "I'm not sure I like the idea of him walking with my brother and sister," Caitlin said, watching much more closely now.

"At least it's not the boy who Marta was caught kissing," Fearghas said, shaking his head.

"Very true. Should we stop him from being with them?" Caitlin's first instinct was to grab her siblings by the arms and make them return to the picnic, even though they'd already eaten their meals.

"I don't think so. We'll just keep an eye on them."

"Mayhap we can get the entire village out here to watch them," she suggested, only half joking.

Fearghas laughed. "Donald is a wild lad. He lost his father, and his mother has four other children. It's hard for her to keep up with him."

"Maybe he should be put into the young soldier program as well. I understand how it feels to have no control over the people you are meant to keep safe."

"Let's give Aileen a little more time there, and I will talk to Donald's mother. Mayhap he can join in another week or two. I would like Aileen to make other friends there before his best friend arrives and turns the world upside down."

"All right," she said. "I trust you." He really seemed to have a knack for parenting that she was lacking.

He interlaced her fingers with his as he looked out over the loch to watch the children who had all stopped walking and stood talking about something in low tones on the other side of the water.

"They're plotting something," Caitlin whispered to Fearghas. "Should we stop them?"

He laughed. "Let's give them some space. If they do something now, I will punish them, and they'll learn that I mean business."

Instead of going off somewhere with Donald, the threesome made their way around the loch. When they stopped beside the blanket where Caitlin and Fearghas were enjoying the last bites of their picnic, Donald said. "It was my idea to start the fire. It was a stupid thing to do, and I should be punished, but please don't punish Aileen. He did nothing wrong."

Caitlin looked at the lad. "He was supposed to be at the wedding feast in the keep. Was he there?" she asked.

Donald frowned. "Nay, but it was all my idea."

"It doesn't matter whose idea it was," Fearghas said. "He was disobedient, and he will accept the consequences. Does your mother know that you were in the woods starting a fire?"

"Nay," Donald said. "I was supposed to be at the feast as well, and with all of us, Mum can't keep up very well."

"Which is even more of a reason you should always be on your best behavior," Fearghas instructed.

"Aye, sir."

"I want to see you behaving properly from this day forth. Otherwise, you'll be joining my army just as Aileen is."

Donald looked at Aileen, who had his shoulders back as if he was proud of being part of the laird's army. "It might be a good idea for me to join," Donald said. "I'll talk to me mother." With those words, he ran off, and Marta sat down on the blanket with her sister and the laird. Aileen followed suit.

"I think the army is the right place for me," Aileen said. "I'm happy to learn to read in the mornings, and I believe it will be a useful skill no matter what I end up doing, but the army is where I need to be. For now at least."

"It's difficult training," Fearghas said. "But it teaches you to be a man, and that's what you need after living with just women for years."

Caitlin wanted to protest, but she could see Fearghas was getting through to Aileen in a way she'd never been able to.

Marta didn't say anything, but she traced the pattern of the plaid blanket they all sat on with the tip of her fingers. She seemed to be deep in thought.

As Caitlin watched her sister, she saw the glaring face of the woman across the way, and she carefully described where she was to Fearghas. "The woman I told you about is on the other side of the loch, just inside the woods. She is looking right at us."

Fearghas looked up and waved. "That's Isla. We played together often as children, but we haven't spoken in a long while. Not since we were both young."

"And there was never anything romantic between you?" Caitlin asked, surprised by his answer. "She looks at me as if I've stolen you from her."

"Nay. You are just looking wrong. Isla and I were never more than friends. We played in the woods some, and her mother would bring her to the keep when she visited my mother. That's all."

Caitlin didn't believe him, but she knew he wasn't deliberately lying. He wasn't seeing things the same way she was. That wasn't at all uncommon. "I'll remember that," she said softly, not wanting to argue in front of her brother and sister. Things were going well, and she was pleased. Besides, as laird of the clan, she needed to show him true respect in front of others.

After the children went to their chambers that evening, Caitlin sat with Fearghas in the parlor, and they simply talked. About everything happening with the children, and whether or not she needed help with anything.

"Your mother is here every afternoon, helping me with anything I need," Caitlin told him. "She's slowly teaching me how to be the mistress of your keep, but she does it all as we sit and darn stockings."

"How does Marta feel about that?" Fearghas asked with a smile.

"She was so very angry at first, but then your mother told her that she couldn't speak to me how she had, and now she keeps her head down and works like your mother and I do. She doesn't like it, which she makes clear, but she does it. I think she's starting to understand that I was just barely older than her when I suddenly had the responsibility to take care of her and Aileen."

"Which is something she should realize. I'm glad she's at least helping as she can."

"Aye. I am as well. She takes me for granted, which makes sense, as I've always been in her life, but she never really saw me as a person until your mother confronted her."

"I'll have to thank me mother then," he said softly, one hand coming out to cup the side of her face. "I think you're pretty special, and I know my family approves of you. I just wish we could get both your brother and sister to acknowledge that us marrying was good for them as well."

She leaned toward him and kissed him, jerking away at the sound of a clearing throat a short while later. "Marta! Do you need something?" Caitlin asked.

Marta shook her head. "No, I just didn't feel like being alone this evening."

"You're always welcome to join us," Fearghas said. "I'm glad you came down."

Marta took the chair opposite the sofa where her sister sat with her husband. "Do we have reading lessons again tomorrow?" Marta asked. At Fearghas's nod, she said, "I think I want to study our country more. And mayhap the family history of the McClains. The story is so odd someone should write it down for future generations."

Caitlin looked at Fearghas, who seemed to be considering. "I think that would be fine. When you are finished, the history of the family needs to be in my hands and no one else's. Mayhap I'll seal it, and it will always stay in the laird's hands. I do like that idea a great deal."

Marta nodded. "I wouldn't share it with anyone else. I just think if I'm going to do it, I should talk to all the different generations of McClains we still have here in the village. I know they heal one another often, but everyone must die at some time."

"According to the future books my family has, it seems as though there will be a very bad bout of the plague in another one hundred twenty years. It will be concentrated in London, but I don't think it will stay in just that area. So they are planning to keep going until then, if they can make it happen. There are days I will go to see some of my older relatives, and even I marvel that they're still alive."

"Mayhap the power of our seventh son will be healing," Caitlin said.

"Mayhap. It's the power that we all seem to want the most. Though it did get a very distant cousin kidnapped at one point."

"Really?" Marta asked. "Why?"

"Another of the clans had a sick laird, so they took a niece of the laird who was just taking over so he would go and heal their laird. At that point, a promise was made among the highland clans that if anyone needed healing, whether they were allies or enemies of the McClains, help would always be granted if someone asked. We've kept our word through the centuries."

"I'm glad there's not constantly someone here to ask for healing," Caitlin said. "Is there anyone even young enough to go at this time?"

"Me grandfather, Colin," Fearghas said. "He has many powers, actually. And one of his brothers, though I can't remember which, also has the power to heal."

"Why does your grandfather have many powers?" Caitlin asked, surprised.

"We're not entire certain, but all of the women from the future put their heads together, and they decided it was because he was the seventh son of the seventh generation of seven sons. All of his brothers had a power, and then he was born with all of their powers."

"I had no idea that could happen."

"The family didn't either. Though we're all thankful for his powers, I'm glad our sons won't all have powers. Imagine how difficult it would have been dealing with seven boys with magical powers and not just one."

Caitlin shook her head. "I have enough trouble with two children who *don't* have magical powers. I can't imagine even one who does have them."

"We'll manage," Fearghas said. "Your relationship with our sons will be much different than your relationship with your siblings."

"I suppose it will. I still worry I won't be able to keep them all from harm."

"But our youngest son will be able to keep the others from harm. You'll see."

Chapter Eight

By the time Fearghas and Caitlin had been married for two months, summer was in full swing. Caitlin learned some about tending the plants that were not as widespread as most. She and Marta learned to cultivate potatoes, corn, and tomatoes, and many other "secret" crops the McClains had for generations longer than the rest of Europe.

They didn't have to be quite so secretive now that the New World and all the crops had been discovered, so it was actually a relief that the New World was known to them.

They no longer had reading lessons, though Alana still came over every afternoon to make certain things were going well for Caitlin and Marta.

One afternoon, after they'd finished watering the potatoes, Marta brought up her desire to talk to the different elderly members of the McClain family and learn all she could from them.

"I think I'm reading and writing well enough I can talk to them now. According to my research, I'll be taking something called oral histories. I'll piece the oral histories together to get my full history of the family."

"Are you certain that's what you want to do?" Caitlin asked. It seemed like such a strange project to embark upon for Marta.

"I need to do something to keep my mind occupied and out of trouble," Marta said with a wry smile. "I think this is the project I need. I can just imagine someone opening my work in hundreds of years to learn the history of their own family."

Caitlin smiled and nodded. "You have my permission to get started then."

"Get started on what?" Alana asked as she walked into the parlor for a bit of darning and to make sure the other women were doing all right.

Marta looked at Caitlin who nodded. "Tell her what you want to do."

Marta slowly explained the project and what she was thinking about doing. "I think it's a good time to interview the elderly members of the McClain family. The family is so unusual that people need to understand where the traditions came from."

"That's a wonderful idea," Alana said. "I can start sending the different couples to the house. Maybe plan to do interviews for an hour every day?"

"I'd like that a lot."

"Our oldest couple right now is Beth and Gavin. I'll have them come and you can interview them and learn all you need to know. Maybe it would be good if they came for lunch. You could have Cook make tacos."

Marta looked at Caitlin who nodded. "You'll really help me?"

Alana smiled. "Of course I will. I think it's a wonderful idea."

"Thank you, Lady McClain."

"Please call me Alana." It was the first time Alana had given permission for Marta to use her first name. It seemed that she was warming up to the girl now that she wasn't so bitter.

That evening when Fearghas came in from training his men, he looked a bit sheepish. "Aileen was injured today. Someone's arrow went awry and went through his arm. He's been healed, but I'm not certain he won't complain about it."

Caitlin's eyes grew wide. "The healing was complete? Do I need to bandage it? Are we worried about infection?"

"And this is why I came ahead of him to talk to you. Do not pander to him. He was injured, and now he's not. There is nothing left to bandage or get infected. It looks as if nothing happened."

Caitlin took deep breaths, trying to calm herself before her brother came in. "Have you added Donald to the younger men's army?"

Fearghas shook his head. "Nay. I was hoping I could take Aileen from you tonight and go and visit Donald and his mother. If his mother agrees, we'll start training him on Monday."

It was Saturday, so that was quite soon. "Will you teach him to read as well?"

"Nay. I don't see the need at this time. If he decides he wants to be a monk or if he has a need later, we'll teach him then."

"I don't think he's going to want to be a monk," Caitlin said. "Marta is planning on starting her project on the McClain family history tomorrow. She wants it sealed and always handed down to the next laird."

"We can do that," Fearghas said with a smile. Behind him the door to the keep opened, and they both looked to see Aileen heading inside. It was all Caitlin could do not to run to her brother, but she kept her face even.

"How was your day?" she asked her brother.

Aileen walked toward her, shaking his head. "I got shot!"

"You did?" she asked. "Where?"

"In my arm! Fearghas had to take me to his grandfather who healed me just by holding his hand over my arm. I didn't believe all the stories about the family until that happened. It was so strange!"

"I'm glad you were healed. I bet you'll be hungry tonight after getting shot."

Aileen looked at Caitlin oddly. "I thought you'd be upset that I was shot."

"If you are completely better, it wouldn't do any good for me to be upset over it, would it?" she asked.

"I guess not. What's for supper?" The fact that he could easily change the subject to his stomach was all Caitlin needed to know the boy really was all right.

"Tacos," she said. She liked the things, but she wasn't convinced they were as wonderful as his family seemed to think.

"Oh, good! They're my favorite."

"Of course, they are." Caitlin shook her head. Her family astounded her at times.

At supper, Marta talked nonstop about her project until Aileen interrupted to tell her he was shot. It felt like they were a real family now, with her brother and sister not acting as if words had to be pulled out of them. They were excited about their new lives.

After supper, Fearghas and Aileen went to talk to Donald's mother while Marta and Caitlin went into the parlor. "I don't know how I'll be able to take notes," Marta said. "There's not enough paper."

Caitlin smiled. "Use one of the iPads. You can make notes on it, and then when you're ready to write it out, you can use paper. Then you'll only need to use a little bit of paper, but the rest of what you do can be erased as necessary."

"That's a great idea!" Marta said, clapping her hands together. "I've never been so excited about doing something like this in my life. Projects always sound like a lot of work that I don't want to do, but this...it feels like it's a labor of love."

"It gives you a sense of purpose. I think it's good for you. I know I became a lot more interested in doing things after Mother and Father died. I had to so we would have food of course, but it also was a way to take my mind off losing them."

"Until the day Alana said that I was being selfish, I had never considered all you were doing to take care of us. Thank you for not just abandoning us, which would have been much easier."

"Where would I have abandoned you?" Caitlin asked. "You're my flesh and blood. It was more important to me to make sure the two of you were healthy and happy than it was to get rid of you. I love you both."

Marta sighed. "I know you do. But it's still a lot of work to take care of us. I never really thought about the fact that you weren't our parent. You stepped into the role so easily."

"The last thing Mother said to me before she died was asking me to make sure you two were taken care of. So that became my life's purpose. You and Aileen."

"And now you're going to have seven sons. It's crazy."

Caitlin nodded. "It truly is crazy."

Aileen and Fearghas hurried into the parlor. "Donald is going to train to be a soldier!" Aileen said excitedly. "I can't wait for him to start learning with the rest of us. Of course, he'll live in the barracks like the other boys, but I'll stay here."

"Would you rather live in the barracks?" Caitlin asked her brother.

He shook his head. "No, I don't think so. I keep hearing stories of different boys putting fish in each other's beds. I do not want to wake up with a fish for a bedfellow."

Caitlin looked at Fearghas who nodded at her. "He does really well, and I think he should stay here in the keep with us. Unless he stops doing well, of course, and then he can stay in the barracks and sleep with fish."

"I don't want to sleep with fish," Aileen said. "They're slimy."

That evening, with both Marta and Aileen in the parlor with them, it felt as if they really had become a family to Caitlin. It was good that she'd married Fearghas, and now her brother and sister were trying to be productive members of the clan and not fighting her authority every chance they got.

Fearghas had his arm draped over her shoulders as they all talked, and they heard four times, in exquisite detail, how Aileen had been shot.

After the two had gone to bed, Caitlin smiled at Fearghas. "I do believe our first son may be on the way soon."

Fearghas smiled. "I'll have grandfather come over tomorrow and see. He can rest a hand on you and know if you're expecting."

She smiled, taking a deep breath. "I would love to know for certain. You won't be disappointed if I'm not carrying?"

He shook his head. "Of course not. I know we're having seven sons, whether we start next week or in ten years. Of course, I'm pretty sure we'll start next week."

"I'd love that. I'm excited to start having our sons."

"I think your siblings would grow up faster if they had a nephew around."

"Or seven."

He chuckled. "In the end, there will be seven. I have a feeling that your brother and sister will be married before all seven are born though."

"Or they'll love living here so much, they'll refuse to leave to marry."

"There are rooms that aren't as close. Those seven bedrooms near ours are for our sons."

"I'm very surprised Marta is taking an interest in a scholarly pursuit. It's not like her to do that."

"I'm sure it's not," he said. "But it's wonderful at the same time. I'm certain the history she writes will be valued by my family for generations."

"I hope so. I love the idea of having it written down. But more than that, I love the idea that Marta will be the one doing the writing. She's a bright girl, and she always has been, but she discovered lads way too soon."

He chuckled. "I'm sure everything is going to be just fine with her. She's a good girl, now that she's got some structure."

"When she first brought it up, I was worried that she only wanted to do it because it would mean she could leave the keep and not be supervised for a while. But it's not that at all. Your mother is going to have the different couples come here and talk to her rather than asking her to go to them. That way she'll still be under my eye, and she didn't even protest. I'm thankful this is a real pursuit for her and not something that she is using to get away."

"I think they're both ready to be helpful to others. Aileen will start learning to shoot in two weeks."

"Please tell me he's shooting with a bow and arrow and not your mother's pistol."

Fearghas laughed, a deep belly laugh that shook the entire sofa. "Eventually, he'll learn to shoot mother's pistol, but for now, it will be a bow and arrow. All of my brothers and I learned to use the pistol, but there's only one, so she is the only one to carry it."

"That makes sense. Is she in danger?"

"Not any longer. Her father hunted her for a while once she'd married father. You know that she stole away in the dead of night so she could keep from being forced into a marriage?"

Caitlin nodded. "That's why I was so surprised when she agreed that we should marry."

"Of course. But she knows the family's secrets cannot be shared with others. And she knew I really wanted to marry you."

"I'm thankful we did marry," Caitlin said. "The help you've given me with the children has been more than I could have anticipated. And I really enjoy the time we spend in bed together. I don't know if I've mentioned that before."

He chuckled. "I don't think you've said it, but your body has a few times."

She nestled closer to him. "Will we have to stop making love if I'm expecting."

"I have no idea. We'll ask grandfather tomorrow."

"I don't want to ask your grandfather something like that!"

"Then I'll ask him when you're not looking," he said.

"That would be better." She sighed contentedly. "Life just seems to get a little better every day," she said. "I do enjoy marriage with you."

"I'm glad you're so happy here," he said. "I was worried when I had to command you to marry me, but I knew I couldn't take the time to court you after you saw me kill the snake and put out the fire."

"I've not seen you use your powers since," she said. "Do you not use them often?"

"Only when I need to," he told her. He held out his hand and used a beckoning motion, and an iPad that was on a table across the room came floating over to them. "Let me show you how to have this device record what my grandparents say so that Marta can listen many times if she needs to."

"It will do that?" Caitlin asked. She could believe anything of the little device since she'd seen her own image stored on one.

He nodded, showing her how to make it work. "Show her in the morning, and I'll send Grandma Beth and Grandpa Gavin over just before lunch. Make sure you feed them!"

"We'll have cook make tacos. I know it's your Grandma Beth's favorite food."

"That and Irish nachos are the two foods my family loves best. I like them too. I especially love potatoes though. I wish we could have potatoes with every meal."

"Are potatoes available in Europe now?"

"I'm not certain. If not now then within the next few years. We can always claim they were brought to us by an adventurer who went to the New World if we get caught with them."

"Good plan. Now, let's go upstairs and make more plans."

He chuckled. "I go to bed with you, and my brain stops working for a good long while."

"I like it that way," Caitlin said, taking Fearghas's hand and leading him up the stairs.

Chapter Nine

When Fearghas's grandfather Colin came by the following morning, he spent three minutes with Caitlin before turning to Fearghas. "You're going to be a father!"

Fearghas's face lit up. "She's healthy? The boy is healthy?"

Colin nodded with a smile. "Of course."

Fearghas left Caitlin, pulling his grandfather along with him. "We don't have to stop our nuptial activities, do we?"

Colin shook his head. "Nay, you don't. Enjoy your wife. If she has problems with morning sickness or anything else, let me know, but she's healthy and so is the bairn."

"I canna believe it's finally my turn to have seven sons."

Colin smiled and nodded. "You picked a good wife," he said softly. "And her brother and sister seem to be doing well."

"They weren't before we married, but I think both now understand how things should be done."

"Good. Send for me if you need me. Or just think to me. You know you don't have to fetch me or send anyone else."

Fearghas nodded. "Aye, Grandfather. Can you distinguish between all the voices in your head so you would know it was me?"

Colin nodded. "I would know." With that, he headed for the front door of the keep, and Fearghas went back into the parlor where Caitlin was waiting.

"You and the bairn are both healthy. He approves of our match."

Caitlin smiled. "That's nice. I only ever really thought about how you and your parents felt. It's wonderful to have your grandfather's approval as well."

"Grandfather won't tell anyone about the bairn until we do. Would you like to tell your brother and sister first?"

She nodded. "I think that would be best. They don't need to hear it from someone else."

"We can tell them at the noon meal today," he said.

"I'd like that a lot." She stood up to kiss him goodbye before he went out to train his men. "Did you ask him about—"

"I did. He said to keep doing what we're doing."

She smiled. "Good. I would hate to stop when we've just discovered the joy it brings us."

He grinned, kissing her once more. "I'll be home for lunch. Grandma Beth and Grandpa Gavin will be here."

"I've already instructed Cook to make tacos."

"Good. Grandma Beth can't seem to live without her daily tacos."

Caitlin smiled. "I look forward to getting to know her better."

"You'll love her. Everyone does. She's from the future, so some of what she says, you'll just have to accept as truth."

Caitlin nodded. "With as often as I've used an iPad, I do know there were people who came from the future. It seems odd that there were four in your family alone, but I will accept it for truth."

As he left for the day, she sat down with Marta to make sure she was ready for her interview with Grandma Beth and Grandpa Gavin. "Do you have a list of questions you'll ask? I'm going to show you how to record the conversation, so you can listen to it over and over and you won't have to take notes."

"Truly? On the iPad?"

Caitlin nodded. "Fearghas told me it was possible, and he showed me how to do it."

"Oh, that will help me so much! I'm so excited to get started. It feels like this is what I'm meant to do."

"And more. You are meant to do so many things!"

"Do you think? I thought I was just going to spend my life being a wife and a mother. I had no idea there was even a possibility of doing more."

"There's always a possibility of more. There are so many books you could read and learn about the world. You don't ever even have to marry unless you want to."

Marta looked down at her hands for a moment. "I'm not sure I want to. I know that seems strange after the way you and Fearghas found me the day of your wedding, but I thought I only had one option in life back then, and that was marrying and having babies. I feel like the whole world has been opened up to me with the ability to read."

"It truly has," Caitlin told her. "I hope you'll do what you want to do. You know you have a home here as long as you need it."

Marta smiled and nodded. "I do know that. And I thank you for all you've done for Aileen and me. After Alana brought it to my attention, I am now fully aware of all you had to sacrifice to be there for us."

"Everything I've done for you is out of love. You know that."

When the door opened, the sisters looked up to see Grandma Beth and Grandpa Gavin. Caitlin got to her feet and kissed them each on the cheek in turn. "Thank you for agreeing to my sister's request," she said. "I do believe her endeavors will help our descendants."

Beth smiled and nodded. "We're excited."

"I'll leave you to it then. I will do some sewing upstairs, and let you all converse without me."

Marta looked at her for a moment as if she wasn't sure she wanted Caitlin to leave, but then she nodded. "We'll see you at the noon meal."

As she walked toward the stairs, Caitlin heard her sister ask, "Do you mind if I record you on an iPad? I would prefer to have every word you tell me, and not just the ones I jot down in notes."

Caitlin was too far to hear the answer Marta received, but she truly believed it would be a positive one.

Upstairs, Caitlin sewed clothes for a young boy. Oh, how she loved the idea of her sons wearing the same clothes their father had worn, but even better, they would wear the clothes she was lovingly sewing for them. It would be years before even her eldest son wore what she was making, but it made no sense not to make the most out of the things she had.

Caitlin sat in a chair in her bedchamber, knowing one day she would hold her children there, and they would get through middle of the night feedings and all their childhood illnesses right there. In the very chair she sat in. It felt right to know her children would be with her.

When it was time for lunch, she wandered down the stairs, finding her sister's face positively beaming with excitement. "Grandpa Gavin remembers the things his parents told him about the family when he was just a boy. I feel like I know so much more about how the family works." Marta grinned at Caitlin. "And Grandma Beth told me about coming back in time and about the seeds that were brought from the future. I feel as though the mysteries of the McClain family are at my fingertips!"

Marta's excitement was reflected on the faces of Beth and Gavin. "It was our pleasure telling you everything we remember," Beth said. "I've never told a story for a more interested audience."

Caitlin smiled. "Learning to read seems to have opened a great many doors for my sister, both in and out of her mind."

Beth laughed. "Reading is a simple pleasure for many in the future. I'm glad the ability to read is giving similar pleasure to your sister."

"Did you read a lot before you came here?" Caitlin asked.

Beth laughed softly, nodding. "I was in something we called a book club. Each of us had our favorite things in romance to read about, and when we came back in time, we were allowed to choose where we would go. I chose Scotland because I had read so many stories about Highlanders finding love."

"Really? Such stories exist?"

Beth plucked the iPad from Marta's hands and flipped to the books on it. "All of those men in plaids are Highland romances."

"I want to read them!" Caitlin said. "Though I shouldn't waste my time."

"Sure you should," Beth said. "I don't think it matters what you read as long as you do. The more you read now, the easier it will be to teach your sons to read and make literature an important thing in their lives."

"Do you think reading should be important to them?" Caitlin asked. "Won't they be warriors?"

"They will. But being able to read always adds such a new dimension to people's lives. What if one of them wants to open a bakery? They need to be able to label their wares as well as price them. That would be very hard to do without being able to write."

"That is true," Caitlin said. "I'll make sure they can all read."

"Also, think of how excited you and Marta are that you can read. They will feel the same, won't they?"

Beth seemed to think it was essential that everyone read, and while Caitlin didn't want to argue with her, she knew she'd lived all her life without being able to read. It was helpful, and she wouldn't deny that, but it wasn't essential to her life.

"Of course, you're right, Grandma Beth," Caitlin finally said. "And I will happily read the Highland romances. Do you have a favorite writer?"

"You can't go wrong with Caroline Lee," Beth told her. "I love to laugh while I read, and even her titles are funny."

Caitlin smiled. "Then I shall start with her books."

At lunch, Fearghas looked happy to be able to host a meal with his grandparents. "Did you give Marta good information?" he asked.

Gavin nodded, surprising Fearghas by being the one to respond. "I told her everything that was told to me all those years ago. I hope she can cobble together as much of the history of our family as possible. I even told of my niece who was kidnapped so they could receive healing for their laird."

That surprised Caitlin, and she looked at Gavin. "Are you a healer as well?"

Gavin nodded. "I am. When Beth and I were first married, we were always being asked to heal someone or other. Remember that?"

Beth nodded, looking at Gavin with a great deal of love. "I remember it well."

Aileen didn't seem terribly interested in the conversation, so he gave the tacos served all of his attention.

"I have a quick announcement," Caitlin said.

Aileen looked up at that, and Marta looked at her with narrowed eyes, as if she was trying to figure out what her sister would say.

Before she could tell them, Fearghas had blurted it out. "We're expecting our first son."

Marta gaped at her sister. "Already?"

"We've been married for two months," Caitlin said. "I'm surprised it took this long."

Beth nodded emphatically. "The seventh son always has children quickly. It's wonderful news!"

"Thank you," Caitlin said, beaming. She was truly excited about the baby.

"Now I can tell others, right?" Fearghas asked.

"Yes, you can tell others. I just wanted my brother and sister to be the first to know."

"Do you need me to confirm?" Gavin asked.

Fearghas laughed, shaking his head. "I forgot your power was healing. I had Grandpa Colin come and confirm this morning. We should have just waited for you."

"Just so you're certain. Did Colin say the bairn was healthy?" Gavin asked.

Fearghas nodded. "He did. And Caitlin is healthy as well."

Gavin nodded. "Remember if he's ever busy, and you need a healer, come see me. I'm old, but I still get around, and I would love to be useful to my clan."

The news of Caitlin's pregnancy spread quickly. Many people came to the keep to wish her the best and drop off gifts for the laird's first son. After supper that evening, Isla came to visit with a sweet bread as a gift. "I thought you might want to have some of the sweet bread we shared as children," she said sweetly, her eyes not leaving Fearghas.

He nodded. "Thank you. Caitlin and I will enjoy it."

"I'm surprised you chose Caitlin and not someone you cared about," Isla said.

Fearghas smiled. "I didn't know Caitlin when we were children, but I've come to care for her a great deal."

Isla nodded her head. "I'll be on my way, Laird. Congratulations on the baby."

While Fearghas saw nothing strange in the visit, Caitlin did. Isla didn't like her at all, and she had no idea why that could be.

Caitlin brought it up to Fearghas and he brushed it aside. "She's always been a bit odd. Now that her parents have died, she lives alone, and I think she forgets how to be around other people."

Caitlin smiled sweetly. "I'm sure that's it." She refused to worry about it if he didn't. He obviously knew Isla better than she did.

That night, while lying in bed, they talked about potential names for the baby. "Robert?" she asked. "I love the idea of naming a son after Robert the Bruce."

"I believe I have an ancestor with that name, who was also a seventh son. You know, when romances are written about our family, the author may title them with the man's name. Robert couldn't work because of that."

She giggled at his words. "So now ye think romance novels will be written about yer family? Not feeling a bit cocky, are ye?"

He laughed. "I know you were talking to Grandma Beth about Highland romances, and I thought how funny it would be if someone wrote about us."

She shook her head. "Can you imagine? They'd have to make up so much because there's not a detailed family history. But there will be. I'm so thankful Marta has taken on that task. She's so excited about it."

"I think she's enjoying the scholarship of it. Now that she can read, she can learn and create with words. It seems that she's found purpose in her life through reading."

"Aye! She told me today that she was sneaking around with boys because she didn't know there was anything else to do with her life than be with boys. Now she wants to be a scholar, not a wife."

"Good for her!" Fearghas said. "I'm glad she's excited about learning. And I would not have a problem if she never married. Learning and doing things with her life could be just as important. I don't think she could travel outside clan lands on her own to learn new things because others wouldn't be as understanding as we are."

Caitlin nodded. "I'm certain she has no intention of doing so."

Chapter Ten

By Monday, Aileen was so excited he couldn't bear it. His friend Donald would be training with his group, and they would learn to shoot. It was something he'd been looking forward to for a while.

As Caitlin watched him go that morning, she knew he was doing what he was meant to do. Before he'd joined the young army, he'd had no direction, and absolutely no discipline. Now that he'd joined, he was a better person. He was able to stand up for what was right and his smiles came more frequently.

Marta spent the morning interviewing, and Caitlin felt that she would be better off just leaving the keep. She had sewed throughout the first interview, but her feet were itchy, and she wanted to walk. Instead of going toward the woods and past the soldiers, she went out and stood by the loch, trying to see how deep she could see into it. The loch had always scared her a bit, because of stories she'd been told about how it had a life of its own at times.

Now that she knew it was her father-in-law who caused the loch to seem that way, she was no longer afraid. She trailed her fingers in the water. She couldn't swim of course, but she could enjoy the water from the bank, and that's just what she planned on doing.

After a while, she stood and walked toward Campbell land. There was a path across fields, and another that took her over one of the hills. She chose to go over the hill, knowing the exercise would be good for both her and the babe.

It wasn't until she was at the top of the hill that she sensed rather than heard someone behind her. When she turned, she saw Isla. "Are you going to see the Campbells?" Caitlin asked.

Isla frowned at her. "Fearghas was supposed to marry me."

Caitlin's brows drew together. "Is that so? He told me that you were childhood friends, but there were no promises between you."

"The promise was between our parents. We were supposed to be married, but when my parents died, the McClains didn't keep their word."

"That doesn't sound like Alana and Duncan. I cannot imagine they wouldn't follow through simply because your parents died."

"You know little about them. You were barely part of the clan before Fearghas married you, and I have no idea what he sees in you. You're carrying a baby that is supposed to be mine!"

Isla's words sent a chill down Caitlin's spine, though the weather was warm, as it was June. "I'm sorry you feel that way," Caitlin said, but she knew she'd spent enough time in this conversation, so she turned her back to Isla and kept walking along the cliff road.

When two hands pushed firmly against her back, pushing her over the edge, she did all she knew to do, and that was grabbing to a tree growing out of a spot between the rocks on the cliff. She clung to the tree, and thankfully found a spot for her feet. She wouldn't last forever, but hopefully, she'd be heard.

She remembered at that moment, that Fearghas had told her his grandfather Colin was able to hear people's voices in his head. Though she'd never even attempted to communicate in such a way, she closed her eyes and thought with all her might about Colin.

"I need help. I'm near the cliff road to the Campbell's land," she thought as hard as she could. She had no idea if he heard her, so she began shouting as well. No one from either of the clans would hear her unless they were walking along the road though.

Her precarious position made her realize she may never see Fearghas again. She worried for her own life and that of her unborn child, but more than anything, she wished she'd admitted her love to Fearghas. She loved him with everything inside her, and she needed him to know it. Why had she waited for him to say the words first?

She threw out her thought to Colin yet again, telling him she knew she wouldn't last where she was for very long, but she needed him to tell Fearghas she loved him.

As she stood with her toes wedged between the rocks, clinging to the tree for all she was worth, she began to sing one of the songs that had been on an iPad that she'd listened to. There was nothing she could do to help herself. She'd already looked for toeholds going up the cliff, but there had been none. No, she needed to be rescued—soon—or she would fall to her death.

Within minutes, she heard footsteps on the road, and they sounded like they were running. She called out, "Help me!"

To her surprise the face that came over the edge of the cliff was Fearghas's. "Are you all right?"

"Aye! I just can't get back up, and I'm not sure how long my arms will last holding onto this branch."

She saw three more faces over the side of the cliff, all belonging to his brothers. Thankfully, he hadn't brought anyone along who couldn't see him use his magic.

Fearghas called to her, "You're going to need to let go of the tree when I say. I will count to three, and when I say the words, you will release the branch. My powers will pull you to me, as long as you are not clinging to the tree."

"I'm afraid!" she called back.

His voice softened. "Of course, you're afraid lass. No one can cling to a tree that is saving their life and just let go without feeling afraid. But you must. Grandpa Colin heard your plea for help, and he's making his way up here, though a bit more slowly than I'd like. He'll heal anything injured, and we'll head back down to the keep. I'm going to start counting. Are you ready?"

Caitlin closed her eyes and nodded. "Aye." He didn't want his son to die anymore than she did. He would save her. He had to.

"All right. One. Two. Three!"

She let go as soon as he said three, fully expecting to fall, but instead she floated up through the air and landed on her feet in front of him. His arms closed around her as she started sobbing.

"I'm glad you had the presence of mind to reach out to Grandpa," he said softly, his hands moving over her back and holding her close to soothe her.

"Is she all right?" asked a voice that was out of breath. She knew it must be his Grandpa Colin.

"Aye, Grandpa. I would like you to make certain, though."

They helped her sit on a boulder beside the road, and Colin ran a hand a few inches away from her body from her head down to her toes. "She has a sprained ankle," Grandpa said. "I can't sense anything else."

"Would you heal her?" Fearghas asked, his voice sounding agonized as he realized how close he was to having lost his wife.

The slight pain in her ankle that she hadn't noticed until Colin had brought it to her attention, immediately went away, as did the fear that had her shaking.

When finished, Colin said, "I don't want her walking back to the keep. She is probably fine, but she was very afraid, and fear weakens us. I'd like one of you on either side of her the whole way back to the keep."

Fearghas moved to her right, he and one of his brothers making a chair of their arms. "I can walk!" she protested, but the men weren't taking any chances.

"We'll take turns carrying you this way. Grandpa, are you all right with the walk down?"

Grandpa Colin nodded. "I'll be fine. I'm just slow moving these days."

"You've earned your days of moving slow, Grandpa," Fearghas said. "If it is too hard to keep walking, sit on a rock, and we'll come back for you once we have Caitlin settled."

Grandpa laughed. "You forget. I can move at super speed or just will myself there. I couldn't do that going up because none of us knew exactly where the lass was."

Fearghas smiled. "I did forget. You should hurry home. There's no need for you to stay with us."

"I think I'll do that," Colin said, and he moved past them, moving faster than Caitlin had ever seen a man move.

"I hated bringing him up with us," Fearghas said, and his brothers all agreed. "It was necessary though."

"It was," the other brother carrying her said.

Within fifteen minutes, she was sitting on the sofa in the parlor of the keep. As the others left, Fearghas sank down beside her, his arm going around her. "You need to be more careful!" he insisted. "You should take the other road next time you want to go to Campbell land."

"I just wanted to walk, but when she walked up behind me, and told me the bairn I'm carrying should be hers, I didn't know what to do. I turned my back to keep walking, and she pushed me. I've never been so frightened!"

"She? There was someone else up there with you?"

Caitlin nodded, closing her eyes. "Isla."

"She pushed you off the cliff? And you're certain she did it deliberately?"

"I'm positive," Caitlin said softly. "She claimed that your parents made a deal with her parents that the two of you would marry, but when her parents died, yours refused to honor their word."

He closed his eyes and shook his head. "You knew something was wrong there, and you tried to tell me. I'm so sorry." He pulled her onto his lap. "Now we'll have to deal with her, but I don't feel you should be left alone yet."

His mother rushed into the keep, stopping at the door to the parlor. "Are you all right? The bairn?"

"We're both fine, Alana," Caitlin said, breathing a sigh of relief. "Thanks to the very thing that made me afraid of this family in the first place."

Fearghas moved her to sit beside him on the sofa. "I'm going to go and take care of our business. Mother, you have your pistol?"

"Always."

"Protect my wife." With those words, he left the keep, and she knew he was going in search of Isla.

Alana sat down beside Caitlin on the sofa. "What happened?"

Caitlin briefly told the story again, this time making it clear she was talking about Isla.

"She was never promised a marriage? I don't know why she would say such a thing!"

"I don't either. But I do believe Fearghas will get to the bottom of the issue."

When Marta popped her head into the parlor, she saw how pale her sister was. "Are you sick? Is it the bairn?"

"The bairn and I are fine," Caitlin said.

"Go and fetch some warm milk and a bite to eat for your sister. Even bread with butter would be fine. Bread with cheese would be better." Alana didn't seem willing to leave her alone, even for a moment.

"Aye," Marta said, hurrying into the kitchen.

"We should have realized the danger of this," Alana said, shaking her head.

"She's been glaring at me since our wedding day," Caitlin said softly. "I told Fearghas about it, but he didn't believe there could be any true danger."

"He certainly knows differently now, doesn't he?" Alana shook her head. "If you'd said something to me, I would have made sure you were never alone."

Caitlin laughed softly. "And that's why I didn't tell everyone. I need time alone."

"I know." Alana was obviously very upset. "I can't believe she tried to kill you. She was always such a sweet child."

It was hours before Fearghas arrived home. Caitlin hoped Isla hadn't been punished too severely. She didn't know how she would have felt in the other woman's shoes.

As soon as he walked into the keep, Alana smiled. "If you're home for the evening, I'll be on my way."

Fearghas nodded. "Thank you for staying with her, Mother." He walked into the parlor and sat down beside Caitlin. "Are you well?"

Caitlin nodded. "I'm perfectly fine other than everyone fussing over me," she said.

He smiled at that. "Isla was sent back to the Stewart Clan. Her mother was a Stewart, so she has family there. She knows she will be shot on sight if she steps onto McClain land again."

"I'm glad her punishment wasn't more severe," Caitlin said. "Though when I think of it as attempted murder of my bairn, I think I should scream, 'Off with her head!'"

"I agree. My brothers did their best to reason with me and keep me from hurting her."

"It sounds like they did their job."

"Two of my brothers and half my army are taking her to Stewart land. She won't be back."

Caitlin felt relief wash through her body. She was glad the woman was gone. "I realized while I was hanging from that tree that I've never told you I love you, and I thought I was going to die before I could. So I'll say it now. I love you and everything about you. You took me from a life of endless work and made me your wife. I shall always be grateful."

He smiled, cupping her face in his hands. "I loved you the first time I saw you. I didn't want to scare you away by telling you. That's why I forced the marriage more than anything. I knew I needed you in my life."

As they kissed, she thought about how much better her life was with him in it. The family she'd thought was strange wasn't so bad after all.

Epilogue

Caitlin and Marta walked along the path to the woods, with all seven boys marching in a straight line before them. Her oldest was twelve, and her youngest, Boyd was three. He had yet to discover his power, but that was fine with Caitlin. It would give him time to be a normal boy.

They were almost to the woods when Boyd stopped walking, and turned to his right where a butterfly had landed atop a flower. He stared at it for a moment, and then next thing Caitlin knew, Boyd was a butterfly, and sitting beside the other on the flower.

Caitlin blinked a few times before turning to her sister. "I think I know what his power is."

Marta laughed. "This one is going to be fun to explain, won't it?"